T0196034

*A journey from an
Alzheimer's caregiver to a new life of
love and support.*

CASEY'S VILLAGE

*It takes a village
for transformation.*

Rev. Sandra S. Hopper R.N.

BALBOA.PRESS
A DIVISION OF HAY HOUSE

Balboa Press books may be ordered through booksellers or by contacting:

Balboa Press
A Division of Hay House
1663 Liberty Drive
Bloomington, IN 47403
www.balboapress.com
844-682-1282

Because of the dynamic nature of the Internet, any web addresses or
links contained in this book may have changed since publication and
may no longer be valid. The views expressed in this work are solely those
of the author and do not necessarily reflect the views of the publisher,
and the publisher hereby disclaims any responsibility for them.

The author of this book does not dispense medical advice or prescribe the use
of any technique as a form of treatment for physical, emotional, or medical
problems without the advice of a physician, either directly or indirectly. The
intent of the author is only to offer information of a general nature to help
you in your quest for emotional and spiritual well-being. In the event you use
any of the information in this book for yourself, which is your constitutional
right, the author and the publisher assume no responsibility for your actions.

Any people depicted in stock imagery provided by Getty Images are
models, and such images are being used for illustrative purposes only.
Certain stock imagery © Getty Images.

Print information available on the last page.

ISBN: 978-1-9822-5541-1 (sc)
ISBN: 978-1-9822-5542-8 (hc)
ISBN: 978-1-9822-5543-5 (e)

Library of Congress Control Number: 2020918259

Balboa Press rev. date: 10/07/2020

Introduction

This story is a compilation of truth and fiction. I am grateful to my bonus mother, Shirley, for the stories she has told me about my dad and their journey with dementia in the last couple years of my dad's life. I am grateful that I was a hospice nurse in my last positions as a registered nurse. The instructions we were given to help care for people with dementia, and their caregivers, has been so valuable to me in caring for my spouse and my mother, and in writing this book.

Casey's Village has been a labor of love that has helped me with my own journey. There are so many books about dementia and Alzheimer's out there. Some of them have helped me. I decided instead of adding another one like those, I would write a story of fiction that tells my story (with the names and situations changed to protect the innocent) to help me through these challenging times, and perhaps give some hope or support to others traveling a similar journey.

I dedicate this book to my beloved spouse, Wes, and to my mother, Ruby Weitzel. Both of them are experiencing dementia, and they are both still living as I write this. I also dedicate it to my bonus mom, Shirley, who lovingly cared for my dad as he traveled his last years with dementia.

Author Sandra Hopper wraps important messages into a dynamic and fascinating story. Each character captured my interest, each sorrow my heart, and each relationship my desire for more. Sandra's writing leads the reader deep into the lives, trials and joys of people just like you and me. She shows us how to move from suffering and loss to allowing the new and its goodness into our lives. —Lynne Cockrum-Murphy, Ed.D., LISAC

Contents

Chapter 1 1

Chapter 2 15

Chapter 3 21

Chapter 4 29

Chapter 5 41

Chapter 6 53

Chapter 7 67

Chapter 8 79

Chapter 9 89

Chapter 10.. 101

Chapter 11 109

Chapter 12 131

Chapter 13 151

Chapter 14.. 169

Chapter 15 183

Chapter 16.. 191

Chapter 17.. 201

Chapter 18 209

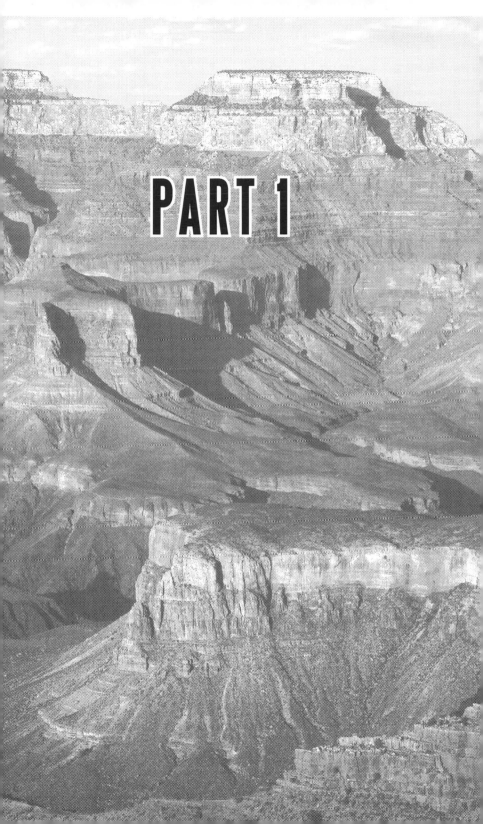

PART 1

Chapter 1

I had no idea as I started my day on that morning how events were beginning to come together to make a drastic change in my life. None of us know ahead of time that changes are about to happen, or we might go screaming out of the picture, afraid of what is to come. Believe me, I would have. Another thing I did not know was how important it is to have the support of others as we go through the changes and find ourselves on the other side. I did not know it takes a village of support.

That day seemed to start out just like any other day for me. My husband was turned on his side, still sleeping. It was not unusual for me to get up earlier than he did. I dressed in comfy clothes, brushed my hair, picked up the book I had started the night before, and then tiptoed out of the bedroom so I would not disturb my husband. I enjoyed having the quiet of the morning to myself.

Do you ever get so immersed in a book you lose track of time and where you are? I loved to read. It would take me away from my life so I could experience adventure, other countries, and romance. All of that had seemed to disappear from my life in the last few years, so I used books to make up for what my life had become. The book I had started the evening before seemed to hypnotize me and had sucked me into the story from the moment I had started it. As I returned to the book, once again I was there, totally immersed in the story, a witness to all that was happening with the characters. The drama had pulled me away from my life to the excitement of revealing who the source of trouble was. It was why I did not hear my husband come into the room, and it was why I was startled back to my own reality when he spoke to me.

Richard said, "I can't seem to talk in the morning," and his words were a little slurred.

Momentarily I thought, *It's a little early for him to already be drinking*, but that thought disappeared. "Don't talk then," I said to him without looking up.

My mother had died a few months earlier, and Richard could not understand why I didn't bounce back sooner after her passing. He thought all our problems were now over, and with my inheritance, and his income, we should have been able to do some of things we had wanted to do. Because things had not happened the way he wanted, he used it as an excuse to drink more than he ever had in the past. His drinking increased beyond the social to where he had a drink in his hand most of the time. Of course, he would deny it if anyone asked him and pretend like he was just drinking iced coffee. I tried to intervene and to let him know I was concerned, but he would laugh me off. He would drink less for a little while, but in a week or two, he was back to drinking excessively. Soon I stopped saying anything.

He went into the kitchen and came back out again. "Casey!" he said loudly. "You need to listen to me! Something is wrong. I'm having trouble speaking, and I can't get a grip on my coffee cup!"

Immediately I moved into action. I threw the book down on the table, and I hurriedly went to get my blood pressure cuff. My husband had a history of high blood pressure, and he had been refusing to go to the doctor to see about getting it taken care of. When I took his blood pressure, I could hardly believe what his reading was. I took it a second time, and it wasn't any better.

"We need to get dressed and get you to the hospital now," I said as calmly as I could because I didn't want to add to the problem.

He refused to let me call an ambulance, so we quickly got dressed, and I drove him to the hospital. I was praying he wouldn't get any worse before we arrived.

After several hours in the emergency room, he was transferred to the intensive care unit. Richard apologized to me throughout the day for putting me through this because he hadn't listened to me and gone to the doctor. I told him over and over, "Richard, what's done is done. We can't go back and change things. I accept your apology."

The neurologist came in, introduced himself, and then sat down with us to obtain Richard's history. He told us the MRI showed Richard had been having mini strokes that neither of us had noticed, or if Richard did, he wouldn't admit to it.

One of his questions was how much alcohol Richard drank, and Richard answered in his usual way, "About one a day."

"Richard," I said, interrupting and glancing apologetically at the doctor, "that isn't true. It's important for them to know how much you drink. Your alcohol intake will affect their decisions about how to care for you." The doctor nodded in agreement.

Richard glared at me and said, "All right, Casey, since you are the nurse, and you know better than I what I do, you tell the doctor how much I drink." He continued to mumble, "That's not true," as I spoke to the doctor about how much he drank almost every day from early afternoon until bedtime. "Casey, I don't know who you are talking about, but it isn't me."

"Well, Richard," the doctor said kindly, "what we will be doing is observing you and treating your symptoms so we can best help you with what is going on. You are receiving medication through the IV now to help bring your blood pressure down. We will start some physical therapy and then some other therapies as we determine what is needed. Right now we are going to keep you on bed rest with a bedside commode. You are in the right place right now to help you with your recovery. Do you have any questions for me?"

"Yeah, Doctor. How long do I have to be here?"

"It's too early to determine that, Richard. It depends on how your body responds to the treatments. We will keep you both informed about what is going on with you. Does that help?"

Richard shrugged. "I guess it has to."

"Mrs. Granger, do we have your telephone number in case we would need to get in touch with you?"

"Yes, I gave it to them when we were in the emergency room."

The doctor read the number to me. "Is that it?" I nodded. "Good. I will be back tomorrow to see how things are going." He shook both our hands.

Richard waited until the doctor was gone, and then he glared at me. "Now everyone will have me labeled as a drunk, thanks to you. I can just see it now at the top of my chart in big red letters. Thanks a lot! Why don't you just go home? I think you've done enough to help me."

"I'm sorry you feel that way, Richard, but I wouldn't have been doing you any favors if I hadn't given them the right information."

"Right according to you, maybe. Just go home."

"All right, I will," I said. I gathered up my purse and leaned over to kiss him goodbye, but Richard turned his head away. I brushed quickly at the moisture that gathered in my eyes. "Have a good night, Richard." He didn't reply.

As I left his room and started past the nurses' station, the doctor stood up and came over to me. "It must have been hard for you to tell us what his drinking habits really are, but I appreciate it. He said something about you being a nurse." He paused, and I nodded. "So you know how important the information is to us."

I nodded again. "Yes, I do know. He's pretty angry with me now, and he told me to go home. I don't really want to leave in case something changes with him. He doesn't understand what his condition is."

"There is a waiting area outside these doors, and for a hospital, they have pretty decent food if you decide to stay. Of course, we do have your number if we need to get in touch with you too. Why don't you take your time to decide what you want to do and then let his nurse know if you are planning to go home?"

"Thanks. I will," I said as I slowly walked toward the doors. I looked back toward Richard's room and then left.

Instead of going to the cafeteria, I decided to go home, take a shower, and pick up some personal things Richard could use while he was in the hospital. I called the nurses' station and let them know I was leaving in case they needed to get ahold of me.

It felt good to be home. I picked up the book I had been reading, put a bookmark in it, and decided I would take it with me back to the hospital. I made a cup of coffee, and I sipped it while I assembled things for Richard. Then I stripped off the clothes I had hurriedly grabbed that morning and took a warm shower. If I hadn't felt like I ought to go back to the hospital, I would have stayed in it longer than I did because it helped me relax.

As I was leaving the house, my cell phone rang, and I quickly pulled it out of my pocket, immediately afraid something had happened to Richard. "Hello?"

"Casey, where are you?"

I sighed in relief as I heard Richard's voice. "I came home to pick up a few things I thought you would need. I was just leaving. Is there anything you want me to bring you that I might not have thought of?" I wanted to add, *"You are the one who told me to leave, so why do you care where I am?"* but I didn't.

"Maybe something for me to read."

"Okay. I will be back in a little while. I love you, Richard."

"Um, I love you, too," he said hesitantly. "There's something else, but I can't think of what it is. It will probably come back to me, and I will tell you later."

I picked up a book I knew Richard had been reading, and I put it in the duffel bag with the rest of his things. As I was walking out to the car, I puzzled over his last comment. It seemed like he had been having trouble keeping his thoughts together lately, but I had put it down to the amount of alcohol he had been drinking.

When I was back in Richard's hospital room, I noticed his blood pressure, according to the monitor, was slightly lower than it had been when he was in the ER. He didn't mention my discussion with the doctor, and I decided I wasn't going to bring it up either.

As I unpacked the bag, I showed him what I had brought. "If there's anything else you want or need, you can let me know and I will bring them when I come back tomorrow."

"Are you leaving? You just got here."

"No, I'm not leaving, Richard. I just wanted to let you know I would bring more things tomorrow if there's something I didn't bring now. How are you doing?"

He shrugged his shoulders. "I don't know. Okay, I guess. I feel kind of groggy, and all I want to do is sleep. Something in the medicine, I guess. I'm glad you brought the book, but I don't know how much reading I will get done. At least I have something more than just trying to find something on the TV." He closed his eyes and dozed off. I picked up my own book and opened it, but I didn't start reading.

The nurse in me looked up at the monitor and read the vital signs displayed there, and I looked at the fluids dripping through the IV. I saw there was an additional small bag of medication, but I didn't want to disturb Richard by getting up to look at it. I knew someone would let me know about the decisions they had been making to care for Richard. I was pretty sure a part of the treatment would be to offset his body's need for alcohol so he didn't go into withdrawal.

Gazing at my husband as he slept, I looked at him as if it were the first time I had seen him. His thinning hair was no longer blond. There were lines across his forehead and at the corners of his eyes. His cheeks were hollow and had a day's growth of beard since we had rushed to the hospital before he could shave. He had stopped exercising, which had always been so important to him in the past. A part of me felt guilty about this because we no longer exercised together or did the activities we used to do. I had been so obsessed with caring for my mother that I had left Richard to fend for himself.

I read for a while, and then it became apparent Richard was probably going to continue to sleep. I was having a hard time staying awake to read, and I decided I would go home. We lived about fifteen minutes from the hospital, so I knew I could be back quickly if something were to change with Richard's condition.

As tired as I was, I thought I wouldn't have any trouble going to sleep, but I tossed and turned, and when I finally went to sleep, it was fitful. I would startle awake thinking I had heard the phone. Finally, toward dawn, I fell asleep. It was the phone ringing that awakened me, and I jumped up to answer it.

"Casey, where are you? I woke up and you were gone."

"I will be back in a little while," I said, attempting to sound more awake than I was. "You were sleeping when I left, so I came home to get some sleep."

"Good for you, being able to sleep in," Richard said sarcastically. "You sure don't get any sleep around this place. This bed is like sleeping on a board, and all of these gadgets make noise. I want to get out of here."

"I don't blame you, but you need to be there until they get your blood pressure under control. You don't want to end up back in the hospital and maybe in even worse condition next time. I will get ready and be back in about an hour," I said, looking at the clock.

He wasn't happy about the length of time it was going to take, but I knew I would feel better after getting a shower and eating something.

Richard was in the hospital for about a week. His blood pressure was stabilized, he was started on some new medication to take at home, and physical therapy had been in to help him with exercises to help increase his strength. His speech was almost back to his normal way of speaking, and he had very little residual weakness in his right arm and leg.

"I'm so glad to be going home," Richard said as we waited for someone to come with a wheelchair to help him out to the car. "I'm perfectly capable of walking to the car. We could be home by now while we wait for a wheelchair."

"Richard, they explained to you that it is hospital policy to have you use a wheelchair."

As I finished speaking, one of the orderlies came with the wheelchair. "I apologize for the wait," he said with a smile. "It seems like a lot of people are getting out of here today. I have your own personal chariot here to help send you on your way."

Richard nodded and sat himself into the wheelchair. "I'm glad you got here when you did. I wasn't going to wait much longer."

When we arrived home, I opened Richard's car door, and then I took the suitcase with his things. "I can carry that," he said, taking it from me. "You don't have to treat me like some kind of baby. I'm fine!"

We walked into the house, and Richard dropped the suitcase inside and walked to his favorite chair. He collapsed into the chair and closed his eyes. "I guess I'm weaker than I thought. Sorry for grouching at you, Casey."

"It's okay. It must be frustrating for you to feel so weak." I picked up the suitcase and took it to our bedroom.

For a few days after coming home, Richard rested. He read books and some of the magazines he enjoyed, and he took naps.

Richard began talking about some activities he would like to do to help get his strength back and get him out of the house. I was determined to join him again. I knew it would help me too.

Richard and I started with walking half a block at a time and then gradually increasing it until we were walking a couple of miles in the morning. It felt good to be out together. We started planning a trip we could take. It had been several years since we had gone anywhere, first because of my work and then all of the responsibilities I had taken on with my mother.

It was like a breath of fresh air to our marriage. We began to laugh again and remember how much we enjoyed spending time together. We had not jumped right into marriage. We had taken several years to develop our friendship before we took the plunge into a deeper commitment. Some people had scratched their heads at how the two of us could even be a couple because in the beginning our interests had been so different. What they didn't know is we each had a deep spiritual desire to be all we could be and to make a difference in people's lives. Richard had done this with his speaking and coaching business, and I had done this as a nurse.

I had allowed the commitment to my own spiritual growth to be derailed as I took on the role of my mother's sole caregiver through the last years of her life. I had made it my priority, and because of this, my spiritual life, my marriage, and every other part of my life had taken a back seat.

Chapter 2

Richard and I decided we would take a camping trip up to the mountains in eastern Arizona for a week. We loved finding a place off the beaten track to enjoy the tall, glorious ponderosa pine trees. I loved to get up close and personal with one of these trees in the morning and to smell its essence in the bark that was like a giant jigsaw puzzle. At night we would hear coyotes calling out, and sometimes we would hear the bugling of elk.

In the past we had invited friends to meet us up in the woods, but this time we decided to make a trip with just the two of us.

Assembling our camping gear, food, water, and the basic essentials became a project for both of us. For the first time, we worked together instead of dividing up the tasks. In the past Richard would take full charge of the camping gear, and I would plan meals, shop, and pack up food and my own clothes. This time, though, Richard was having trouble making decisions about what we needed to take to camp out. I realized working together was a necessity so we would have all we needed for our week in the woods.

It was late in the morning when we found a spot on the rim away from the main roads without any other campers in sight or sound. I breathed in the fresh air, looked up at the blue sky dotted with puffy clouds, and heard the crunch of pine needles and pinecones under foot.

"This is what heaven has to be like," I said to Richard.

"I agree," he said, putting his arm around me. "We need to do this more often and not let life take us away from spending time in nature."

We worked together to raise the tent, pump up the air mattress, and spread out our sleeping bags. Then it was time to set up the kitchen area with a propane stove, folding tables, a lantern, ice chests, and a large container of water we would use to wash dishes.

"Our home away from home," Richard said. "This was a good idea. I'm glad we decided to come. How about some lunch, and then if you want to, we could go for a hike?"

I was really glad we had brought Richard's handheld GPS and that I knew how to use it because when we started back toward camp after several miles into the woods, Richard lost his bearings and wasn't sure which way we needed to go to return to our campsite. I gently showed him on the GPS where we were and the direction we needed to go.

My own panic wanted to take over as I began to realize this wasn't some kind of joke but that Richard really was having trouble with his memory. Richard had been camping and bowhunting most of his life, and he had always been well aware of where he was at all times. I was comparatively new to this outdoor life, so it had not come easily to me. But Richard had been a skillful, patient teacher. Thank God I hadn't decided he could be in charge of that part of our hikes. I had realized I needed to be able to take care of myself in case something would happen to either of us while we were out hiking. Now it had.

"I don't know what was going on out there," said Richard after we returned to camp, and as he sat down in one of our lawn chairs. "I guess I didn't realize how tired I was after the drive up here."

"That's probably it," I replied, but inside, I questioned if that was the truth.

We enjoyed our time together but decided after four days we would pack up and go home the next day. Richard had lost confidence in his ability to be able to take off and hike by himself as he had in the past. I was relieved not to have to be in camp wondering if he was okay, and if he would be able to find his way back to camp.

On the final morning of our camping trip, we decided to get everything packed up and then to stop for breakfast in one of the small towns on our way home.

"I'm sorry for cutting the trip short," Richard said after the waitress had left us to place our order. He took a sip of his coffee. "I know you would have liked to stay longer."

I shook my head. "No, I'm glad we decided to leave. It looked like some storms might be headed our way, and being cooped up in the truck or in the tent all day would not have been my choice. This way we are left with wanting more, and we can look forward to our next time. Maybe then we will invite Suzy and Bill and some of the others to join us. Although, I did enjoy having our second honeymoon with just the two of us."

"Me too. You've been a good sport about all of this, Casey, and I want you to know I really appreciate it."

One day a few weeks after the camping trip I came into the living room, and Richard was sitting on the sofa with tears running down his cheeks. He looked up at me and said, "I used to be able to go into the woods, and I never got lost. You know that. Now I am scared to death that I will get lost. I hate being like this. You expect it when you start getting older, but I'm not even seventy."

I went to him and motioned for him to stand up. I put my arms around him, and he wept. "I love you, Richard. It sounds so painful to me. I wish I could do something to change things."

"Thank you for being here for me, Casey. I really appreciate you and love you so much."

18

We didn't make time for any more camping trips after that. Richard made up a story he told to our friends about me not wanting to do any more camping unless it involved a hotel and reservations. At first I denied saying it, but then he would assure me I had said it, so I quit trying to defend myself. Richard decided there was no reason to hang onto most of our camping equipment, so he gave away everything except for our sleeping bags.

Chapter 3

"That was fun," I said as Richard and I were loading the dishwasher after some friends of ours left our home.

"I didn't think so. I would have much rather sat and talked than play cards."

I had noticed Richard having difficulty making choices about which cards to play, and his inability to remember, or to even seem to care, about how to play the game. His partner had been patient with Richard, but it was challenging for him to watch his wife and me win several games in a row.

"I can finish this, Casey," Richard said, indicating the dishes waiting to go in the dishwasher. "You have been busy the whole day cleaning and cooking. Go put your feet up, and I will finish the dishes. It's the least I can do after you put all of this effort into making a nice dinner."

"That's really sweet of you. I appreciate it." I picked up a magazine I hadn't had the chance to look at and settled into my favorite chair in the living room.

After finishing the magazine, I decided a cup of tea would taste good and returned to the kitchen. Richard had left the kitchen to go into the family room to watch television. I had heard the dishwasher running, but I had no idea that soap suds were pouring out of it until I went back into the kitchen. Forgetting all about making tea, I quickly ran to the dishwasher and turned it off. I didn't want the drying cycle to start and make it even worse by cooking the soap on to everything in the dishwasher.

On TV it had seemed funny when Lucille Ball would do something like this, but I failed to see the humor. It took me an hour to remove everything, rinse them all, and then to clean all of the soap out of the dishwasher. Richard came into the kitchen as I finished mopping up soap off the floor.

"I wondered where you had gotten to," he said. "I thought maybe you had gone off to bed. What are you doing?"

"We had a small disaster, but I have it all taken care of now. The dishwasher was putting out soap suds, so I needed to clean things up."

Richard accepted what I said and only said, "If I had known, I would have been glad to help you, Casey." There was no reason for me to lay guilt on his head about what had happened, so I let it go.

"I know you would have. I'm pooped out, and now, I am going to bed."

***

"Richard, I didn't sleep very well last night," I said the next afternoon as I gathered up dishes from our lunch. My busy mind had been mulling over the incident with the dishwasher and other things that had been happening with Richard. I had been awake a good part of the night, and I felt sluggish and achy. "I'm going to take a nap."

Half an hour later I woke up to what sounded like an explosion, and a terrible smell wafted into the bedroom. I jumped up out of bed and ran into the kitchen. A small pot was on the stove with the remnants of some boiled eggs, and there were pieces of egg splattered on the cabinets near the stove, all over the stove, and some on the floor and vent hood. Richard was nowhere to be seen.

I quickly turned off the stove, and with a potholder, I took the pot off the stove to cool off.

"What happened here?" Richard asked as he walked into the kitchen. He looked at the mess, and then at me. "I'm sorry, Casey. I put the eggs on to boil and then went into my office to get something." He took my hand and walked with me to the door leading out to the patio. "It's nice out here. I will bring you a glass of iced tea, and you can relax. I will clean up my mess."

It was a pretty day, so I wandered around the yard admiring our pretty flowering plants scattered among cactus that are native to the desert. I was grateful to have someone coming in once a week to do yard work since it was too much for me to handle with all that was going on with Richard now.

I sat down on one of the benches, and the tears started to flow. There was beauty all around me, but I felt so alone. We had no children together, and Richard's son, Norman, had not been a part of our lives for many years. The one good thing I had noticed, with all that was happening, was the change in Richard to a softer, kinder person, who demonstrated his appreciation and gratitude to me for being there for him.

I decided in that moment to get an appointment with the neurologist Richard had seen in the hospital when he had his stroke. I wanted clarity about what was happening, and to see if there was anything that would help.

When I went back into the kitchen, Richard had finished cleaning up most of the mess. He had been focused on it and hadn't remembered to bring the tea, but I didn't mind. The forgetfulness was part of what had become a part of our lives.

***

We saw the neurologist, Dr. Johnson, and he ordered some tests to be done. A month later we went back to Dr. Johnson's office to find out the results. He confirmed what I had already been thinking. Richard's diagnosis was Cardiovascular Dementia and Alzheimer's. There was also evidence Richard had been having small strokes.

"So, what do we do now?" Richard asked. "Is there some kind of cure or medication?" Richard was holding my hand, and he squeezed it as we waited for the answer."

"There is no cure," Dr. Johnson answered. He took off his glasses, and his voice was kind, as he continued. "There is medication that may help with your memory that I will order you." The doctor also reassessed Richard's other medications.

"I would advise keeping your brain active with puzzles or working on the computer. A great organization that can support you is the 'Alzheimer's Association.' They can answer a lot of the questions that you may have, and they have support systems for both of you."

***

One day I finished some housework, and I sat down to read for a while before starting in on my next project. Richard came and sat down next to me. His mouth was turned down, and his eyes were sad.

"What's going on, Richard?" I asked, putting my arms around him.

"I feel so insecure because of the Alzheimer's. It's like having pieces of my brain missing. I don't know from one moment to the next what is going to happen. I hate feeling this way."

There wasn't much I could say, but I held him and stroked his back. "I am so grateful you are here with me, Casey. I don't know what I would do without you, and I feel bad about what you are having to go through because of me. You are an angel."

"We are a team, Richard. You have always been here for me, and I am glad to be here for you."

He returned the embrace and then dropped his arms. He turned the television on and said, "I'm going to see if there is anything on, and if not, maybe I will take a nap."

***

"What would you like to eat, Casey? I'm hungry," Richard said as he opened the refrigerator. "Did you have something planned? I don't see anything."

One of the ways Richard had won my heart was by cooking. He had been single for so much of his life that he had taught himself to cook. We shared cooking our meals, and it was a lot of fun for both of us. Cooking was one of his skills that I had watched drop away, with sadness.

"I didn't go to the store today. You could make us some fried egg sandwiches?"

Richard looked at me without moving. It was almost as though he didn't comprehend what I was asking.

"How about if I help you, Richard? We can work on the sandwiches together."

He grinned. "Yeah! I like that."

I retrieved the ingredients from the fridge and took the frying pan out of the cupboard. He put bread in the frying pan, and I removed the bread and handed it back to him. "How about you put this in the toaster, and I will get the eggs frying?" I pointed to the toaster.

It turned out to be a slower process than I could have imagined because I needed to give him step-by-step instructions. Richard continued to smile, and I was grateful I hadn't just taken over and did it by myself. I realized making the sandwiches without him might have been easier but would have robbed us of the joy of creating our dinner together.

Chapter 4

At first, I would talk to my girlfriends about what was happening with Richard, but then I quit. Some would offer me their sympathy and say things like, "I know what you are going through. We went through the same things with my aunt before she died."

It only made me want to scream at them and say, "You didn't live with her, so you don't really have a clue," but I didn't. I began to stuff my feelings down and not share with anyone what was happening except for a very few people.

Richard had one friend who remained fiercely loyal to him and would call him several days a week to stimulate him with politics and whatever was going on in the world. Richard and Bill had been hunting buddies since before Richard and I met. When Bill and Suzy had gotten married, Richard had been Bill's best man. Richard was not much of a hunter, but he had loved getting out in nature and spending time with Bill. Suzy and I would roll our eyes when the two men would start in about some of their hunting stories, but we laughed and enjoyed our time together.

As Richard's memory impairment increased, I began to isolate even more. It became harder and harder to leave him at home by himself even to run to the grocery store, and I started thinking, *I'm sure people are tired of hearing me feeling sorry for myself.*

One day Richard said, "Casey, I think we need to see our lawyer to update our will. I want to make sure everything is in place to help you."

"Okay. I will give her a call and set up a time."

I made the appointment for the next week. When I reminded Richard about it on the day of the appointment, he asked, "And why are we going to the lawyers?"

"We talked about it last week. You mentioned you wanted to make sure everything is up to date."

He shook his head. "I don't remember, but that doesn't mean it didn't happen. This Alzheimer's messes me up. If I didn't have you to help me, I don't know what I would do. I hate being such a burden on you, but I'm grateful you are here."

"Richard, you aren't a burden. I love you very much. We are a team," I added as I put my arms around him.

I was grateful we went to the lawyers, and I was grateful Richard had suggested it. Our lawyer understood what was happening and made some suggestions of things to add to our will that we had not had on the original one.

"Richard, how about we stop for a cup of coffee and a piece of pie? We aren't that far from Aunt Sally's Café."

"I would enjoy that," he answered.

We drove to the café and then walked up to the door together. It wasn't that busy because it was after the lunch crowd and about an hour before the café would be closing for the day. Customers would order at the counter, and then waitresses would bring the food to the table.

Richard looked at me, and said, "You just order something for me, Casey. You know what I like. I'm going to go sit down."

I ordered something for both of us and then went to join Richard at the table he had chosen.

"This is a nice place," he said as I sat down. "I'm glad we came. We haven't been here for a long time. It was a good idea. We haven't been getting out very much."

"We haven't. I thought since we were close by, it would make a nice treat for us."

"This place isn't really in our neighborhood, although I like it. What made you choose it, rather than something closer to our home? This is a long way to come for coffee."

"I thought since we were over here to see our lawyer anyway that we could stop here and do something different rather than just go home. You have always enjoyed their pie in the past."

Richard looked puzzled. "We went to the lawyers." He shook his head and then tapped his head. "I had forgotten we went there. This Alzheimer's. I can't remember anything. I hate it."

I squeezed his hand, and just then our server brought our order.

***

One day I decided to take a walk around the block to clear my head. I was ready to turn onto our street when I saw a man ahead of me going in the opposite direction and realized it was Richard. I hurried to catch up with him.

"Richard," I said, breathing hard from rushing, "where are you going?"

He stopped and looked at me as if he weren't really seeing me and then whispered, "I'm going home. Can you help me? I don't know where my home is."

I started to put my arm around him to offer him some comfort, and he pushed me away. "No. Don't do that. I don't know you! Don't touch me! I just want to go home!" he said, shouting at me.

Panic rose within me. I wasn't sure what to do. What would I do if I couldn't convince him about who I was and where he lived? I had even left my cell phone at home, so I didn't have any way to call for help, although at that moment I didn't know who I would call.

"Richard," I said as gently as I could, "it's me, Casey. Your wife."

He looked at me and hesitated. "I want to go home. Can you take me home?"

I started to turn him in the direction of our home, and he protested, "No, not there. I want to go home."

"Where is home, Richard?" I asked gently, not wanting to set off his anger.

"Forty-eight hundred Wilshire. I know it's just down and around the corner."

"Richard, there isn't anyone there now," I replied. "You haven't lived there for a very long time. You live over here with me. We've lived here for over twenty years." He looked at me with watery eyes, his confusion evident. "Come with me, and I will make you some lunch, and you can rest for a while. You must be tired after all of this activity." I continued taking my time as I spoke, and he was finally willing to take my hand and walk to our home.

That night I was sleeping when I was awakened to some tapping. Rat-a-tat-tat. Groggily I wondered what that was, and then I heard it again. It seemed to be coming from the front door. I reached across the bed, and it was empty. Now I was fully awake. Could that be Richard? I turned on the bedroom light, hurried to the living room, and turned on the outside light. I could see through the window that indeed it was Richard. He was standing outside dressed in his pajamas. His feet were bare.

I opened the door, and Richard tapped out the rat-a-tat-tat again, a big grin on his face.

"Richard, what are you doing out here? It's cold outside," I said, stating the obvious. "How about coming in and I will make us some hot chocolate?"

His smile widened, and he accompanied me back in the house. I noticed that neither the door nor the screen door was locked, so he could have come back in the house on his own. It was then I knew I had to do something to make him safe and so I would hear if he opened the door.

We enjoyed our hot chocolate and then headed back to the bedroom. After that experience, I wasn't sure I could go back to sleep, but I did.

Caring for Richard was much different than it had been when I was my mother's caregiver. He was much younger and stronger. She had been in an assisted living apartment so I could go home after several hours. Taking care of Richard, I had no place to go. It was no longer safe to leave the house, so I had groceries delivered to the house and had the mail delivered to our home, along with his medications. I cut both of our hair. Shopping was all done online, although I didn't do much of that. There wasn't anything I wanted or needed. I napped when he napped, because he would get up and wander around the house in the middle of the night. I lived in fear that somehow, some way, he would make it out of the house or yard, get lost, or get hit by a car.

Richard's symptoms with his Alzheimer's increased faster than many other people's did because he continued to have small strokes. He lost the use of his left hand, and his left leg was weak. He had to start using a walker, and then not too long after that, he was using a wheelchair. Richard would try to tell me something, but he wasn't able to come up with the words to get his message across to me. I did my best to interpret and read his mind to figure out what he was saying, but I was not always successful. He would hit the side of his head in frustration, his eyes filling with tears, pleading with me to understand.

When Richard was no longer able to communicate or to care for himself at all, Richard's friend Bill suggested to me that I might think about calling to see about having hospice come in. It surprised me that I had not thought about this myself, because of my nursing background, which had been in the clinics at the Indian Health Hospital predominantly. I called Richard's doctor, and a nurse came out to assess Richard to see if he was eligible to start hospice.

I was relieved when the admission nurse with hospice was able to set up having a nurse, social worker, chaplain, and nursing assistant come to help out with Richard's care. They encouraged me to care for myself, but I no longer was sure what that would look like.

Richard had only received hospice care for two months when he died. He had quit eating about a week before, and he was sleeping most of the time. I would sit at his bedside reading, and I would moisten his mouth. No one was home but me when he died. I had gone into the kitchen to have something to eat, so I wasn't at his bedside when he took his last breath. I was grateful hospice personnel had told me Richard might decide to pass away when I was out of the room. Otherwise I probably would have been filled with guilt for him dying alone.

I cleaned out the house after the memorial service. I gave his clothes away to an organization that gave clothes to homeless people, and I donated our furniture to a thrift store. I started to box up a few things of Richard's to send to his son but decided since his son had decided not to be in the picture for years that he wouldn't care about Richard's belongings. The last thing to go was our home, which sold within a few weeks, and then I moved into a small apartment.

People from hospice had warned me not to make any life-changing decisions for at least six months after Richard died, but I couldn't stand the thought of being in that house, surrounded by over twenty years of history.

Now I was alone.

PART 2

Chapter 5

As I stood about two feet from the yawning canyon, I looked down at the scuffed end of my cheap running shoes. My little toe was peeping out the end of one shoe. It was a laugh to even think of these as running shoes. The soles were so thin traction didn't exist, and the insides were worn down, without any kind of support. I barked out a harsh comment: "Like I need running shoes anyway. Who knows when the last time I went for a walk, much less a run." A brief memory passed quickly through my thoughts about how good It had felt when I did run as I had hit my stride and finally obtained that runner's high. Some call it bliss. I shook off the memory. "Useless!" I muttered. "I'm not that person anymore."

I raised my eyes to focus on my surroundings. The day reflected back my own gloom. The canyon was in a gray shroud of low overhanging clouds. The colors were muted. Was it sending me an invitation to carry out my plan? I was there because I had held the Grand Canyon as sacred for most of my life. It seemed like the appropriate place to give my final offering.

In the distant past, Richard and I had rafted down the river and hiked its trails. Sometimes we were with a group, and other times we had gone as a couple. They were some of the happiest times of my life.

All of that was over five years ago. Now Richard was dead. All of our dreams were dead. There was nothing and no one in my life. I was alone. I felt like I was already dead.

I had chosen this particular place where I was standing because it was a sheer drop. There were no ledges that would break my fall. I did not want to end up on some outcropping partway down still alive in a broken body. I wanted a clean jump straight to the bottom.

It was quiet. The shuttle I rode to this isolated vista had left, taking the other tourists back toward the beginning of the route. Another shuttle would be arriving soon. On that cold, sunless day there were fewer tourists willing to brave the elements, which would provide a smaller chance of witnesses as I carried out the completion of my plan.

I moved closer to the edge. I realized I was overthinking what I was doing. For months it had been this way. I felt like I was constantly moving through molasses. Everything took effort. *Why can't this be easy just to do the deed? I'm such a coward*, I thought.

I took a deep breath, fiercely attempting to close out my traitor thoughts. With my eyes tightly closed, I started to move forward. My heart was beating wildly in my chest, and because of the thundering of my pulse in my ears, I could not hear anything.

As I put out my foot to take the last step, I gasped and started to struggle as I was grabbed from behind and pulled away from the edge of the canyon. I screamed, "What are you doing? You have no right to interfere with me. Let me go!"

My attempt at battling this intruder was useless. I felt like a rabbit caught in the talons of an eagle. I couldn't remember being so angry and terrified at the same time. As soon as I felt the constraint lessen, I started to run away, but a strong grip on the back of my sweat shirt stopped me.

"Let me go!" I choked out, and then I was horrified at myself as I started to cry, unable to stop myself as the emotions I had been storing up began to let go.

The hands that had been gripping me gently turned me around and then gathered me close, like a wounded child. My head was pillowed next to a wool-covered chest. I had stiffened, and then like a balloon deflating, my tears started leaking from my eyes and then increased into a torrential flow.

Large hands patted me on the back, and a rough voice murmured close to my ear.

I don't know how long we had been standing there with my cheek pressed against his chest when I realized that a stranger was holding me. I started pushing away, beginning to imagine how awful I looked with my red, puffy eyes and runny nose. I had always hated what I looked like when I cried. I was afraid to look up.

A neatly folded white handkerchief was handed to me. "Here you go. It's clean."

I looked at the handkerchief for a moment, not wanting to spoil it with my snotty drippings.

"Go ahead," he urged me. "That's what it's there for."

I wiped at my eyes and blew my nose and then for the first time dared to look up at the man who had now prolonged the inevitable. Deep brown eyes gazed at me with such kindness and compassion that my own eyes started to water, and I bit my lip to prevent the waterworks resuming. My voice shook and was barely a whisper as I said, "Thank you." I couldn't believe how sore my throat was now after releasing the emotions I had been storing for so long. "You shouldn't have stopped me," I said hoarsely. "I will just do it some time when you aren't here. Maybe not today, but I will jump."

I expected his demeanor to change from kindness to anger. I expected his eyes to grow cold with irritation. I expected the gentle smile to disappear. But none of this happened.

His brown eyes twinkled. The lines in his face that were a product of laughter and good humor appeared, although he didn't laugh. He rubbed the bushy mustache under his nose.

He pulled at his beard without speaking. Slowly he shook his head. "Somehow I don't believe it," he said softly. "I think you want to believe it," he emphasized, "but I do believe inside of you there is a place that is relieved you aren't lying at the bottom of this canyon as a heap of bones and blood.

"What do you think, Peter?" he asked turning to his companion, who I hadn't been aware of until the question was asked. My rescuer turned back to me and explained, "Peter is my husband, and I have never known him to lead me wrong about something as important as this."

I turned toward the man called Peter. Peter was the opposite of his husband in outward appearance. Peter was about two inches taller, slender, with long runner's legs. He wore hiking boots, corduroy pants, and a blue quilted, down jacket. His hair was covered with an orange and blue knitted cap. The blue of his jacket and cap matched the color of his eyes.

"I agree with Jacob. It looked to us like you were having an argument with yourself about the whole thing." His gaze was compassionate and gentle. "We watched you for a minute or so, before Jacob moved to stop you." Peter's eyes misted over, and his chin wobbled slightly as he continued, "We had someone close to us jump from this same spot a year ago."

Jacob reached out, put his arm around Peter, and kissed Peter on the cheek. "I hate to see you hurting, babe."

Peter nodded. "It isn't just me, Jake. We are both hurting." Peter sniffed, took a deep breath, and continued speaking to me. "We weren't here to stop him. Nobody was here to stop him. The person was our son, Jeremy. He had just returned from Iraq after three tours."

Something twisted inside of me. Viscerally I felt the pain of these two men, this couple who had reached out to stop me. I nodded. "Seeing me here brought it all back to you. I am sorry I have added to your pain. I want to thank you for being here for me despite your own circumstances. You have helped me a lot. I'm all right now." I looked at my watch, which wasn't there, and frowned. I had left everything in my car. "It's time for me to leave and let you have your time here."

I started to move away, and Jacob and Peter simultaneously shook their heads. Jacob spoke first. "That is not a good idea. You need help."

Peter nodded in agreement. "You may think you are okay now because you have released a lot of emotion, but the reasons that brought you here today are still there and need to be dealt with, or as you said a few minutes ago, you will come back and finish it when we aren't here," Peter said, and Jacob agreed.

"Come with us to the lodge. We can have a meal and talk," said Jacob.

I pushed my fingers through my short, ratty hair I had cut myself. I was suddenly very aware of what I looked like with my oversized sweatshirt, big T-shirt, and baggy jeans that all had seen better days.

"I can't go in some place like that," I said. "I look like a bag lady right off the streets of Phoenix. They probably have some kind of dress code, and this isn't it." I added with embarrassment, "I didn't think I would need to wear something acceptable to others when I came here, and I didn't bring any other clothes with me." The truth was I had given away my clothes, my furniture, and everything else, because I knew I wouldn't need them anymore, and I didn't want to leave a mess for my landlords. My lease was up, and I had handed in my keys a week early without any explanations to anyone.

Seeing my dilemma, Peter nodded. "It doesn't matter to me what they might think at the lodge, but I understand it does to you. There's a diner not too far away where you may feel more at ease."

"That's a good idea, Pete. It's a place where hikers and campers and tourists of all kind gather. Nothing fancy about it, but it does have pretty good food. It will be my treat. By the way, you know our names now. What do we call you?"

"Casey. My name is Casey."

The restaurant was cafeteria style, so after we selected what we wanted, we took seats in a corner booth away from the other patrons. Jacob removed the trays, and I stared at the sandwich and fries in front of me, not knowing how to start. Compared to what my companions had chosen, the food on my plate wasn't much, but it was more than I had been eating for months.

"Aren't you hungry?" asked Jacob as he started to take another bite of his hamburger. "We can get you something else, if you want."

I shook my head, picked up one of the fries, and then took a careful bite. "I haven't had much of an appetite lately.

"It shows, Casey." Jacob lifted up my left arm. "I don't know what your normal weight is, but I doubt this is it. You are pretty much skin and bones," he added kindly. "I don't mean to pick on you. I want to express my concern for you. It definitely looks like whatever drove you to want to end your life today wasn't something that just started a few days or weeks ago." He gently placed my arm back on the table.

I put my hand in my lap and then looked from Jacob to Peter, and then back to Jacob. My eyes watered, and I sniffed back tears. I definitely did not want to start crying again. "It's been going on for some time, and I don't have the energy or the desire to change things or do things differently. I'm a mess. There is nothing anyone can do to fix me."

"There are people who can help you, Casey. Jacob and I have had help dealing with Jeremy's death. It may all feel pretty hopeless right now," Peter said, "and I assure you getting help can change your life around by giving you a different perspective and hope." He had taken off his cap, and his thinning blonde hair had been played with by static electricity. Peter had been patting at it while he had been talking to me and finally shrugged and left it alone.

"Would you allow me to call a friend of ours for guidance about what the next best step would be for you to get that help?" asked Peter.

I placed my head in my hands. I felt numb. I didn't know what to say. I had already said more to these two caring people than I had to anyone else in months. I fought back tears that were wanting to come again.

Peter moved to sit next to me on my side of the booth. He put his arm gently across my shoulders and briefly hugged me. "Whatever you decide for yourself, I want you to know Jacob and I want the very best for you. There is hope."

"Okay, you can call your friend," I whispered shakily.

"I'm going to take the call outside," Peter explained, "where there is less noise and more privacy. Why don't you try to eat something, Casey, if you are able?"

I watched Peter make his way through the restaurant. I wondered what I was letting myself in for by agreeing to have

Peter speak to his friend. I frowned and looked down at my plate of food that was practically untouched.

"This must be scary for you, Casey, and I want you to know how courageous I think you are for trusting a couple of strangers to hand out suggestions about how you can do things differently." Jacob softly laughed at his own words. "Suggestions might not actually be an accurate word since we have kind of been ordering you around."

I shrugged, not really knowing what to say, and bit into the sandwich. It tasted like sawdust. Just the bite was hard to swallow, so I put the sandwich back on the plate. Jacob continued to eat and ignored my futile attempts.

Peter had made arrangements for me to be picked up and to have my car towed to a storage place near the hospital. I would ride by medical transport to a hospital in Flagstaff and then probably be transferred to another facility that specialized in mental health challenges. I had agreed to all of this, but the longer we waited for everything to transpire, the more doubts started to seep in. I had no idea if I was making the right decisions. Everything had seemed so simple earlier, and now it was complicated.

Peter and Jacob had convinced me doing things this way was the best way because driving myself would give plenty of time to rethink my decisions and to change my mind, which already seemed to be happening.

I was scared. I decided for this moment I could hold onto their belief that taking these steps could change the direction of my life for the good.

While we were waiting, Jacob and Peter walked with me to my car, and I retrieved my purse and water bottle. I had brought nothing else with me. Each of them attempted to distract me by pointing out some of the wildlife that walked around, seemingly undisturbed by the tourists milling around.

"Thank you so much for helping me, Jacob and Peter. I appreciate it, no matter what happens," I said when my ride appeared

"You'll see, Casey," Jacob said as he enveloped me in a big bear hug. "Things are going to be different for you now."

"I hope so," I said shakily.

He took my chin into his hands and looked directly into my eyes. "Remember, believe in our belief for you until you can believe for yourself." I nodded.

Then Peter took me in his arms. "We will be checking in with you to see how you are doing. Our friend Georgia will be waiting for you at the hospital, so you won't be alone."

Chapter 6

A van came with comfortable seats that reclined. The driver didn't expect conversation from me, and I was glad. I was exhausted after the turbulence of emotions I had finally expressed. I curled up in the seat and went to sleep.

A couple of hours later I was gently awakened by someone patting my shoulder. It was hard for me to rouse myself out of sleep. I felt very disoriented as I tried to figure out what was going on. It had been a long time since I had slept so deeply.

"Miss, we are here," I finally heard and understood we had arrived at the next step of my journey.

Fear spread through me. I had no idea what to expect, and I started to regret allowing myself to be persuaded to come here. I knew Jacob and Peter thought this was the best thing for me, but I was not convinced. Then I remembered Jacob's parting words, "Believe in my belief until you can believe it for yourself." I closed my eyes and took a deep breath.

I whispered, "I will believe in Jacob and Peter's belief in me, because I don't have that belief for myself. In fact, I don't know what to believe."

I stood at the outside of the emergency room doors hesitating when a petite woman with curly, brown, shoulder-length hair approached me. "Casey? Hi, my name is Georgia. Peter and Jacob are friends of mine. The ER people are waiting for you, and if you will allow me, I would like to stay with you so you won't be alone."

"I don't know what to expect," I said hesitantly. "Usually I would be the one expecting patients. I'm not used to being 'the patient."

"I didn't know you have a medical background. Peter didn't say anything about it."

"It wasn't something we talked about."

"A new experience for you, and I realize it doesn't necessarily make it easier for you. Being on the patient side of the process is different, and it can be kind of scary. That's why I want to be with you. You will be making the decisions yourself. I will be here as your advocate and support team. What do you think?"

I looked into her almond-shaped brown eyes, and I could see the warmth and caring. "I would like that, but it seems like I'm taking advantage of someone who doesn't even know me. You probably have a lot of other things you could be doing other than helping a crazy person out."

"Casey," Georgia said firmly, "it is my choice to be here for you. It doesn't matter that until a few minutes ago we had never met. I feel like it is a real privilege for me to be here to support you. And as far as you being crazy, that is not true. What I see, and what Peter and Jacob saw, is someone who has been battered by life's experiences and is at a crossroads of finding a new direction for her life. You may not see it now—in fact, I'm pretty sure you don't see it now—but if you are willing, there are people who can help you. It is up to you."

Tears started leaking out of my eyes. Georgia put her arms around me, "It's going to be all right, Casey. You will see. You are courageous—" I started to interrupt her, but Georgia continued, "You are courageous. You wouldn't be here now if you hadn't had the courage to listen to Peter and Jacob, and then come here. You may have a hard time believing that about yourself now, and I hope one day in the not-too-far future you will be able to claim it for yourself."

"Jacob and Peter told me to believe in their belief until I could believe it for myself."

"Good advice. I'm right here believing in you too." She hugged me and then led me to the admission desk.

Georgia was true to her word. She stayed with me through the admissions process. I stumbled over the questions about my address because I no longer had one. I would look over at Georgia, and she would nod and squeeze my hand to reassure me. If she hadn't been there, I would have bolted for the nearest exit. It was so painful to admit I was alone, and I had no place to go. I had made sure of it as I had planned my exit from this life.

I was grateful for the people handling my admission because none of them acted surprised or judgmental about how I answered the questions. They accepted my answers as if it were an everyday occurrence for someone to show up with no address and no emergency contacts.

When the questions were answered and my vital signs measured, Georgia and the nurse escorted me to a patient room in the emergency room. As we walked down the hallway, my senses were assaulted by the noise of humanity. Babies were crying, I could hear someone moaning, and there were urgent movements in and out of one room by different personnel as they cared for someone in crisis. All of the rooms were on the outside of a large circle with the nursing station in the middle. I wanted to hide in a corner away from the noise and sights.

"Ms. Granger," a nurse in blue scrubs said with a gentle smile, "I need you to change into this fancy gown and pants." She handed me a patient gown and bottoms. "And here is a bag for you to put your own clothes into after you change. The doctor will be in shortly to examine you." As she was leaving, the nurse pulled the long privacy curtain across the glass door and then shut the door behind her.

"Can you manage changing by yourself, Casey?" asked Georgia. When I nodded, she added, "Okay. I will step out of the room and give you some privacy. I will be right outside. You can let me know when you are ready for me to come back in with you."

As the door closed, I was suddenly alone for the first time since I was pulled to safety by Jacob and Peter. It seemed so quiet and foreign to me, even though I had been in hospitals and medical establishments most of my life as a nurse, and then as a caregiver to my mother and my husband. Rarely had I been on the receiving end of the medical world.

After stuffing my clothes into the plastic bag the nurse had given me, I went to the door and invited Georgia back in. A part of me had been afraid she wouldn't be there, and I would be all alone again, but she was there, as she had told me she would be.

I sat on the edge of the bed, and Georgia took a seat in a chair close to me. "I was afraid you wouldn't be there," I admitted, my shoulders slumped, my head hanging down, and my fingers pleating and then smoothing the light blanket I was sitting on.

"I hear you, Casey. You may have experienced people leaving you and/or not keeping their word with you in the past, but I'm not one of those people. I am here for you. You will also find other people who are willing to support you too. Just think," she said with a gentle chuckle and a squeeze of my hand, "today alone you have three new people in your life who care about what happens to you."

I nodded, and my eyes filled with tears. I swiped at the moisture with the edge of my gown, and Georgia handed me a tissue. "I can't believe I'm crying," I said impatiently. "All I have done today is cry. It isn't like me. I can't remember the last time I cried before, not even when my husband and my mother died. It was such a relief that they were no longer suffering. I felt guilty for not being able to cry, and I thought, *People must think I don't care that they are gone, which isn't true. I have no idea what I am going to do with them gone.*

Georgia gave my hand a squeeze and spoke to me with gentleness. "I'm glad you are now in a safe place to let those feelings loose, Casey. It is a part of the healing process to let go of what was and to move forward toward a new life, a new way of being. People don't always understand if we don't grieve in the way they think we should. The truth is, everyone grieves differently, and grief takes as long as it takes."

"Knock, knock," a male voice interrupted. A man with a clipboard and papers in his hand moved the curtain aside and then stepped into the room. "Sorry to interrupt. I'm Dr. John Webber." He came forward and shook my hand and then Georgia's. "Have we been treating you all right so far?"

I nodded as I looked up at him.

"It looks like you could use some water. They wait to bring it until I give them the okay, so I'll let them know when I go out to the nurse's station." He lowered himself onto a stool with legs. "Can we talk about what brought you here today?"

I looked over at Georgia, and she nodded her encouragement to me. "Yes," I answered, glancing at him and then down to my hands. I twisted my fingers together nervously. "I tried to jump off a ledge at the Grand Canyon this morning, and some people stopped me. They stayed with me and then talked to me about the importance of getting some help." I gestured in Georgia's direction. "And they called Georgia to see if she could help me."

"Are you all right with Georgia being in here while we talk?"

"Yes, please. It helps me a lot to have her here. Is that okay with you, Georgia?"

Georgia said, "I'm glad to be here to support you, Casey."

"Do you still want to kill yourself, Casey?"

My eyes filled with tears. "People keep telling me there is hope for me, but I'm having a hard time believing it. I really don't know what the best thing for me is. It seems like dying would solve a lot of problems. I don't know that I have what it takes to keep on living."

"There is help available to you. I am grateful the people who helped you today, including Georgia, have been there for you. What I need to do is a brief physical—get some blood drawn and some x-rays—and then I would like to have some intravenous fluids given to you to help you get hydrated. Then we will find the best place for you to receive the care you need. How does that sound?"

I shrugged my shoulders. "Okay."

When the doctor finished and the tests had been done, I lay on the bed watching the clear saline drip into the tubing and down to my arm, where the intravenous needle had been inserted.

"Georgia, thank you for being here with me. I must be keeping you from your own work."

Georgia shook her head, and her curly, brown hair bounced on her shoulders. "I have a light day today, and I am glad I am able to be here with you."

"What kind of work do you do?" I asked, glad to take the attention away from myself.

"I am an associate minister of a church. My responsibilities are mainly with pastoral care helping people to get the care they need, and I work with our chaplains to give them training and support." She noticed as I started to frown. "I'm not here to convince you to come to our church or to convert your own beliefs, Casey. I'm here to support you and be with you, as I said before."

I waited a moment before answering, and my words, when they came, were defensive. "I haven't had anything to do with church for a long time. I used to consider myself pretty spiritual, but somewhere along the line I've lost my faith."

Georgia nodded and didn't seem shocked or repelled by my words. "I'm not surprised you feel that way. You've been through a lot and have had a big burden on your shoulders."

"How long have you been a minister?"

"I was ordained about ten years ago, and I've been at our church for a little more than five years. Before I attended ministerial school, I worked as a social worker and really loved the work I was doing with people."

"How did you end up becoming a minister then?"

Georgia laughed. "I was eating breakfast with my partner, and all of a sudden the words started tumbling out of my mouth about wanting to become a minister. It shocked my partner, but I was also shocked. I had not consciously been thinking about it at all. The next thing I knew, I made arrangements with my minister to find out what I needed to do next, and as they say, the rest is history."

"Did you ever regret your decision?"

"When my partner decided being with a minister wasn't what he wanted for his life, and then he moved out, I started having doubts. Later when I started to prepare to move closer to the school I would be attending, which is located across the country, I started to have second thoughts. It didn't help my confidence when some well-meaning people questioned me about leaving a job I had been good at and loved.

"But in my heart of hearts I knew this was the right decision for me, and that if I didn't do it I would regret it for the rest of my life."

"Wow! That took a lot of courage, Georgia."

"It did, and I am so glad I went through with my decisions. What I do now has brought me an even greater sense of fulfillment than I had when I was working as a social worker."

I was alone in the room after persuading Georgia she should leave to get something to eat and to do whatever she needed to do for herself. She had been with me constantly for three hours, and I felt bad that she was glued to my side for so long. She had left me her telephone number in case they started making arrangements for my transfer to another facility before she came back.

I relaxed, and my mind started to wander back to what had truly framed the events of this day. My mother's face was vivid in my memory as I remembered who she had been before Alzheimer's had claimed her, and she shriveled into someone I could barely recognize any more. Mom had always enjoyed hiking and camping, accompanied usually by her dog, Princess, and some of the people she had worked with. I had admired her greatly for raising me alone. She had always been there to support me. When Alzheimer's robbed her of being able to function independently, then I knew it was time for me to step up and care for her.

Richard could understand, at some level, my desire to care for Mom, but he didn't want her to move in with us. Fortunately for him, my mother had no desire to live with him either. If it had just been me, she would have come to live with me in a heartbeat.

Mom moved into an assisted living apartment. All her meals were provided for her, along with weekly housekeeping. I felt bad because she adjusted poorly to that move, and she ended up isolating herself from the other residents. They provided activities, but she refused to participate. I felt guilty about her being so alone, and I started spending several hours almost every day with her, which didn't help Richard's attitude at all. I didn't listen when well-meaning people would tell me to stay away for a little while to help her get used to her new home. I couldn't stand the thought of her being all alone.

After about a year of living there, Mom's memory deteriorated even more than it had. She would ask me the same things over and over again. This woman who had always been a spotless housekeeper would leave dishes all over the apartment, would leave the coffee pot to burn dry, and had stopped taking showers. She looked like a wild woman with her gray hair standing out from her head and wearing clothes that were stained and unwashed. When she had first moved in, Mom would take her clothes to the laundry room to wash and dry and then would spend hours ironing them neatly. I started doing her washing and ironing while I was there, or I would take them home with me.

"I don't know why I'm still here, Casey. I'm not of use to anyone," Mom would say frequently.

My answer to her was always, "I don't know why either, but I'm grateful you are here, because I get to spend more time with you." It was hard because I knew this was not the life my mother wanted, and it was painful to watch her decline.

I knew other living arrangements were soon going to be necessary for Mom's safety, and I dreaded having to make those decisions. I should have known Mom would retain some of her independence to the end, and one morning she didn't wake up. I received a call from the facility letting me know that when they went in to give her the morning medications, my mother had died in her sleep.

I made the arrangements for Mom as if I were in some kind of trance. There weren't a lot of decisions to be made because Mom had everything written down, and I was her only living survivor.

I should have been grateful she was no longer living the life she had hated as she realized she was losing her memory.

It was painful to watch and listen as she berated herself for forgetting.

After my mother's death, my days became long and uninteresting. It was like caring for her had sucked the energy right out of me. All I wanted to do was nap or read. It certainly wasn't the retirement I had envisioned when I had left my nursing position with the Indian Health Service where I had worked for over thirty-five years. My husband and I had both dreamed of traveling abroad, and maybe even living overseas. There were opportunities to volunteer that we would have both enjoyed, but it just seemed to take too much effort to think about, much less to plan and do.

Chapter 7

I must have dozed off because I jumped when Georgia came into the room. "Hi, Casey, I'm back," Georgia said cheerfully as she stepped back into my room. It took me a moment for my heart rate to slow down. "I'm sorry, I didn't realize you were sleeping. I didn't mean to startle you."

"It's okay. I'm glad you are here. I didn't even realize I had fallen asleep."

"I'm glad you got some rest. Has anyone come in to talk about what comes next?"

"No," I answered, "and I admit, I have no idea what to expect. They have been in to check on the IV, and to see how I'm doing, but that's all." Without realizing I was doing it, my fingers started busily pleating and smoothing the blanket that covered me.

Georgia was about to reply when the doctor came back into the room. "Mrs. Granger, how are you holding up?" He paused and then continued. "Your lab tests are back, and they show the dehydration I suspected when you arrived, and you are a little anemic. We will finish the fluids that you have running now. It's important for you to be drinking water and to eat. Any questions so far?" He waited for me to shake my head. "We have made arrangements to transfer you to a behavioral health facility to get help for your mental health. Unfortunately, we don't have any open beds here, but where we are sending you they are experts on the care you need right now."

I nodded as I listened to him, and I took in a deep breath. I looked over at Georgia, and her smile encouraged me. "Okay," I said. I felt the heat in my neck and face. "I never thought I would be on my way to a mental hospital. It's so embarrassing."

"I imagine it might be," the doctor said kindly, "but they will help you move through this." He shook my hand and then Georgia's.

Georgia came over and gave me a hug. "You are finishing a chapter in your life, Casey, and ready to start a new one. Remember what Jacob said—to believe in his belief for you until you can believe it for yourself? I want you to know, I also believe in you, and you can believe in my belief for you until you are ready to believe it for yourself.

"They won't allow me to come with you or to visit right away," Georgia continued, "and I want you to know I will come when they will let me." She handed me a business card. "This has my number on it. You can call me. I spoke with Peter, he gave me his number and Jacob's number, and I wrote their numbers on the back of the card. They said you can call them too. We are all rooting for you, and we want to keep in touch with you."

Tears trickled down my cheeks, and Georgia handed me a tissue. "Thank you, Georgia. I really appreciate all of you. I guess I will call you my Three Musketeers."

"Sounds good," Georgia said, grinning.

It was a short ride to the behavioral health hospital, but it seemed to take forever. I felt like I was in a goldfish bowl with the whole world looking in as I rode on a gurney in the back of an ambulance. I had helped to transport patients by ambulance in my early days as a nurse, but this was my first, and I hoped the last, as a patient.

The first night and most of the next day I was in an observation room filled with matching recliner chairs I could sit or lie back in. There were about twenty other people being observed also. Far from being a restful environment, it was a place of noise and light 24–7. Some of the people did not commit quietly to being in this place of locked doors and personnel watching us all the time. One young man was screaming and swearing to be let out. I tried not to pay much attention, as I made myself as small as possible. I did not feel safe at all, and I was longing to get out of this place. I thought, *If you weren't crazy when you came in here, you would be before you left.*

I was interviewed by a psychiatric nurse practitioner in a small room away from the noise and confusion. She ordered some medications for me that were supposed to help me, but nothing would have helped me while I was in that observation room except for being induced into a coma.

During those hours, I thought about how I had felt afraid that nothing was ever going to be different than it was. Little by little I had stopped going out to be with friends or to go to church.

When hospice came in to help for the last two months of Richard's life, I was grateful. They offered so much, but I didn't know how to accept it. I had been doing his care for so long that I didn't know what to do with myself while someone else bathed him. I did accept weekly visits from a volunteer, and I was able to do grocery shopping without fear something would happen with Richard while I was gone. I went grocery shopping, but by then, neither one of us was eating very much.

I had been told to take care of myself, but I had no idea what that meant other than taking a shower and brushing my teeth. Food didn't appeal to me, and my clothes hung on me like they belonged to someone else. I avoided looking into mirrors, not wanting to see the ghost of the person that was reflected back to me. I would take scissors and chop off my hair to keep it off my face and so I didn't have to do anything with it. It had begun to be just something more for me to take care of, so I hacked at it instead of going to get it cut and styled.

Finally, I heard my name called, and someone came to escort me from the observation room to another part of the facility. It all seemed so foreign to me. We had to wait for the door to be unlocked from the other side before we could enter. It became obvious to me that you had to have permission to go from one part of this place to another.

"Hello, Casey," a tall, slender woman with gray hair greeted me. Her smile was friendly. "My name is Lisa. Let me take you to your room. You will be sharing it with Gina for now."

I followed her to a room across from the nurse's station. One twin bed was rumpled, with the sheets and blankets carelessly pulled up to the top, and clothes were thrown helter-skelter on the low dresser and bed. It reminded me of what a teenager's room might look like. On the other side of the room was a neatly made bed with a stack of towels on the end of it.

"Here is a place for clothes," my escort said. "You can have family members bring some for you. This way is to the bathroom." She guided me to a closed door just inside the entrance to the room. Inside was a sink, toilet, and shower with places to hang towels. My roommate's towels were already hanging there, and a toothbrush and toothpaste were on the shelf next to the sink. "Not very fancy, but it will handle your needs." She handed me a small plastic bag, which contained simple toiletries, and I was glad since I didn't have anything with me.

We left my new room, and Lisa continued the tour. "Group is just getting started. These meetings are an important part of your recovery, and I would advise you to take advantage of them."

She opened the door to a large room, where people were already gathered in a big circle. Some people looked over at me, and some either had their eyes on the leader or were looking down at their feet. The one thing I noticed is that most of the group were a lot younger than I was, and I seemed to be the oldest person in the room. Apparently when most people have mental problems, they start a lot younger than I did.

"Marge, I want you to meet Casey," Lisa said to the woman leading the group. "Marge is one of our staff, Casey. I will leave you in her capable hands."

Marge smiled, and she pointed to a chair close to her in the circle that had a spiral-bound book on it. "Nice to meet you, Casey. The book is for you, and you might say it's your new Bible, for now. We use it in our group sessions. It will be a good resource for you as you deal with life in all its ups and downs. Since it is your first group, you don't have to share this time, unless you want to, but I would encourage you to participate in upcoming sessions. Participation is a key element to progress."

I nodded in response, and then my eyes followed around the circle as the other people gave their first name so I could start getting acquainted with them. My new roommate was sitting across from me with her legs pulled up under her. Her long brown hair was pulled back in a ponytail. She smiled and gave me a wave. "Hey, roomie."

When it came around to me, I said my name, and then other than following along in the book, I didn't contribute anything else to the discussion. I didn't see how any of these younger people could relate to what had brought me here. Most of them talked about problems with their families or school.

The next day I was pulled out of the group in the morning to talk to a social worker, and I talked to her about being literally homeless and not having any clothes to wear, other than the ones I had worn to the hospital originally. My wardrobe now consisted of the hospital-type pajamas the facility had given to me. She assured me that together we would find solutions.

After that group session, the nurse, Lisa, came to find me. "Casey, we have some clothes that may fit you. Sometimes people leave clothes behind." She handed me a couple of pairs of jeans, two blouses, and some underwear. "Nothing fancy, but at least they will get you out of the hospital garb."

"Thank you. I appreciate it."

A tall, slender man with his hair pulled back in a short ponytail approached me. "Hello, Casey, I'm Dr. Rosh. Would you please come with me to my office?"

Dr. Rosh interviewed me and gave me a short test, and then we decided on a treatment plan to help my symptoms. He added a medication to the antidepressants, which had already been ordered for me, to help with anxiety.

"We will see how you do with these, Casey, and change them if we need to."

Little by little a weight seemed to be coming off my shoulders, as I started to participate and share some of my story in the group meetings. I had been right about them not really understanding what I had been through, but what these young people did was listen to me, and they verbalized how proud they were of me for speaking up. I had to use a pay phone to call anyone, and I was shy at first about calling Georgia, Jacob, and Peter, but I was glad I did.

"Casey, I can hear in your voice some excitement," Georgia said. "Every time we talk I hear changes, and I'm so happy for you."

"I didn't see how being here could help anything, but it has," I agreed. "The social worker showed me some places online today that are for rent. I don't want to buy anything right now. Would you be willing to accompany me to look at them, Georgia?"

"Thank you for asking me. I would love to do it."

The next day Georgia and I headed out on our mission to look at possible places for me to live. I had obtained a list from the social worker and had called to make appointments to see them.

Georgia had suggested we take a detour first, and I thought it was a great idea. We stopped at a salon she used to get her own hair styled.

"I'm nervous, I have to admit," I said to Georgia. "My hair is a mess from me chopping at it. I doubt if they will be able to do much with it."

She laughed and squeezed my hand. "I think you will be pleasantly surprised."

The stylist greeted Georgia with a hug and then turned to me. "Casey, it's so nice to meet you. I'm Kelly." She had long, slender fingers, and she gently ran them through my hair. "Do you have an idea of what you would like for your hair? I love the texture, and I think doing some conditioning will help it a lot."

"This is a nine-one-one visit. I don't know what you can do with it, Kelly. I would just like to be able to go out in public without frightening small children," I said with a laugh.

"There's not any danger of that," she responded. She led me over to the shampoo bowl and started washing my hair. I couldn't believe how good it felt to have someone else wash my hair, and then she ended with massaging my neck, and I was almost purring.

"Maybe all I came in for was the hair wash and neck massage."

"I love giving my customers a little extra love." We walked over to her station. "I'm excited that you are putting your hair in my hands. I will talk to you about what I'm doing, so if there is anything you don't like, let me know."

Half an hour later, Georgia and I left, and I felt like a new woman. I was amazed at how Kelly was able to shape and even out my hair. It was the first time, in a long while, that my hair was shining and styled in an easy-to-care-for way. Kelly had shown me how to apply gel and to then run my fingers through my hair to allow it to have a carefree look. I no longer thought I would have to color my salt and pepper hair for it to be something I would like to see reflected back to me in the mirror.

"Your hair looks sassy," said Georgia, and I gave her a hug.

After leaving there, we stopped at a boutique, and looked at some clothes with some style that would also be comfortable to wear and would actually fit me. I was grateful for the clothes that had been donated to me when I entered the hospital, but I knew it was now time for me to have my own clothes.

It was fun shopping with Georgia, and the sales lady joined in on the fun, bringing other things for me to consider. When

I left there wearing a pair of lavender jeans, a white tee shirt with small lavender flowers, and a lavender jacket, I was grinning like a little child who had just spent time with Santa. Both Georgia and I were carrying bags with clothes, and not all the clothes were mine.

We left there laughing to go to our first appointment to see an apartment. I walked into the place with confidence, knowing what I wanted. I realized as we walked through it that it didn't have the character I was looking for. It was pretty basic, but it left me wanting more.

A couple of blocks away, I saw a sign for an open house. It was a small, older home with a large shade tree in front and a covered porch that invited you to come and rest for a while.

"Georgia, would you mind if we took a look? We have some time before we need to be at the next place."

"Let's do it."

I walked in the front door, expecting something totally different. The space had been remodeled, and it had an open concept, with the kitchen separated from the living room by an island. I barely listened to the friendly real estate agent as he guided us through the place. The only bedroom had a large window looking out into the garden, and the bathroom was just off it with a walk-in closet.

"Georgia," I said, as we sat back in the car, "I don't need to look anymore. I can see myself right here. It might sound kind of crazy, but I knew as soon as I walked in the front door I wanted it. So much for me just renting for a while," I added, laughing.

"I don't think it's crazy at all," Georgia said, laughing along with me. "I would call it a God job. It is no accident that this is the first day they are showing it, and you were the first person to see it."

We called the places where we had appointments to cancel and then walked back into the house, where the realtor greeted us.

Chapter 8

When I left the behavioral health facility a few days later, I had not closed yet on the home I was buying. Peter and Jacob invited me to stay in their guest house. At first I was hesitant, but then I decided it would make a nice transition from the fishbowl of behavioral health, where there was always someone there, before moving into my own home. It would also give me time to find the furniture and things I would need.

In the guest house, I had everything I needed. I didn't see Peter and Jacob every day, but it wasn't unusual to share an evening meal or brunch on Sunday. The guest house was in back and to the right of the main home, and it was connected by a beautiful yard and covered patio.

I returned to my meditation practice, which had once been an important part of my life. I had allowed it to slip away when life's circumstances had intruded, and a part of me started blaming God for letting it all happen. I felt calm and centered for the first time in years, and I was grateful I had put meditation back in my life. I knew it was what kept me calm and in control of myself when I received an unexpected phone call from Richard's son.

I had been living there for about two weeks when I realized it was Richard's birthday. It was his first birthday after his death and another first for me to experience after someone dies.

I went to the store and bought the things I would need to fix Richard's favorite meal of shrimp and pasta. I decided this was the way I would wish him a happy birthday.

After the meal, including a piece of double chocolate cake, I took a glass of wine out to the patio. It was a beautiful, quiet evening. I could hear birds and the buzz of some insects. It was so peaceful. I took in a deep breath and closed my eyes for a moment, taking it all in. I became aware of how grateful I was to be alive and felt at peace.

My cell phone rang, and I looked at the caller ID, frowned when I saw the name, and considered not answering. I knew, though, that it would be better to handle whatever it was about rather than putting it off.

"Hello, Casey. I thought, seeing how it's my father's birthday today, that I would give you a call." The words were slightly slurred, and I could hear the clink of ice in a glass after he finished speaking. "Oh, sorry, I should have said, 'Hello, Casey, this is Norm,' since it has been quite a while since we have talked. You might have not recognized my voice."

"Even if I hadn't recognized your voice, Norman, I do have caller ID, so I knew who was calling. What's up?" I asked coolly.

"Cut right to the chase, huh? No small talk. No asking me how I'm doing or what it's like living here in Atlanta. What's up is that it is my father's birthday."

"I am aware it is. I wasn't expecting your call. How nice of you to want to remember him on his birthday."

"Well, it's not like I don't remember him other times too. He was my father, after all, even if he didn't do such a great job of being my father. He didn't care about me, which really showed up when all he left me was a damn dollar when he died. What kind of a father does that?"

"Norman, we've been through all of this before. Goodbye." He started to sputter out a protest, but I ended the call.

Tears leaked down my face, and I brushed at them with my fingers. "What am I crying about?" I asked myself. And then I laughed and took a sip of my wine. "That's Norman in full character. Poor baby! At fifty-five years of age, he is still making Richard the cause of all his unhappiness and failures. How sad is that?"

I closed my eyes and took another deep breath. I opened my eyes and looked up at the sky. It was a beautiful clear evening, and I could see stars twinkling. It was another reason to be grateful. Living north of the city and away from all the city lights, I was able to enjoy the night sky.

I saw Jacob come out of his house, and I gave him a wave.

"Hi, Casey. Would you mind some company?"

"No, please join me."

When he sat in a chair across from me, Jacob said, "Are you okay? I don't mean to be interrupting."

I shook my head. "You aren't interrupting. Today is Richard's birthday, and his son called to remind me of it." I laughed harshly. "I did good! I practically bit off my tongue to keep from telling him off. I'm well aware it's Richard's birthday, and in fact, I cooked Richard's favorite meal in order to celebrate. The thing is, when Richard was alive, Norman never called unless he wanted something and never made a point of calling on Richard's birthday. I, frankly, was surprised he even knew when his father's birthday was. All he really wanted to do was gripe because his father only left him a dollar when he died. Our attorney had suggested it when we set up our wills, because we were afraid Norman would try to fight the will."

"Wow, girlfriend!" Jacob said, clapping his hands. "I'm proud of you. I'm afraid I would have not been so kind to him if it had been me. You did good."

I smiled and lifted my wine glass in a toast. "I did do good." My eyes became moist, and I swiped at them. "The thing is, Jacob, I could have really used his support when things got so bad with Richard's memory. Dammit, Richard could have used his support! No one who hasn't been there to actually experience someone going through dementia, and the pain it causes them and their family, has a clue as to what it is like.

"Richard did what he could to deal with the disease progression when he was aware of what was happening. He was grateful I was there supporting him. Then there were other times he would lash out in anger because he couldn't remember, and he would blame me if something wasn't where it was supposed to be.

"One day I found him sitting in our walk-in closet holding his head and crying because he couldn't think. It was painful to witness the pain he went through."

Jacob listened, reached out and took my hand, and gave it a gentle squeeze.

"I'm sorry for dumping on you, Jacob. I do have my therapist I've been seeing every week that I have been able to share these things with, and for that, I am so grateful."

"Please don't apologize. Your Three Musketeers, which I am proud and grateful to be a part of, continue to be amazed about the courage you have shown in going through all of these things to get your life back. I'm happy to give you a listening ear when you need one."

"To not only get my life back, but to get a life I had forgotten was possible. I am grateful to you, Jacob, to Peter, and to Georgia. Each one of you has been amazing. All of you have chosen to support and nurture someone you didn't know eight months ago. I feel totally blessed. I know not everyone has the support system I have."

"Knowing you, Casey, I have no doubts you will be paying it forward to other people. In fact, from some of the stories you have told us about from your group therapy sessions, you already have been there supporting other people."

"Thank you. I appreciate you saying that. Would you like a piece of Richard's birthday cake to help me celebrate? If Peter is around, he is welcome to some too. Double chocolate cake ..."

"Say no more. I will go get him, and we let the party begin."

***

I was coming into the yard from running some errands when I heard my name.

"Hi, Casey, Jacob and I have some salmon and roasted vegetables we're serving in about an hour. Are you interested?"

"Sounds delish. What would you like me to bring?

"We've got it handled."

"Thanks, Peter. Other people's cooking always sounds delightful. I appreciate the invite."

When I walked into their home a little later, the aromas coming from the kitchen had me salivating.

"Here," Jacob said, handing me flatware and napkins. "The food is all just about ready. I opened a bottle of white wine. Is that okay for you?"

After dinner was completed and the dishes done, the three of us went into the living room. It had been raining, so the temperature outside had dropped. Sitting close to the fireplace where a fire was crackling and popping felt cozy. I picked up a photograph album that had been placed on the coffee table.

"I don't remember seeing this before," I mentioned.

"We've had it tucked away," said Jacob, "and just brought it out a couple of days ago. This is an album Peter and I started when Jeremy first came to us. We were having a hard time looking at it, but now we want to move past that and enjoy the memories, right, Peter?" Jacob added.

Peter nodded. "It is time to celebrate the years we had with Jeremy. Watching you tackle your challenges has helped us to be able to deal with our own loss. Would you like to see some of the pictures?"

"I would love to, and thank you for being willing to share with me. I'm grateful if my struggles have helped you. Both of you have helped me so much."

The three of us sat close together on the sofa, and we opened the album. The first page showed a toddler with dark, curly hair, bright brown eyes, coffee-colored skin, and a big grin.

Peter gently put a finger on the photo. "This was the day he came to us. He was such a happy little guy considering all he had gone through. His mother was a young addict who took her own life, and we fostered him while they searched for family members who might be able to take him. We were his foster parents for almost a year, and no one in the family came forward. We petitioned to be able to adopt him. In those days it was a big deal, really a miracle, for a gay couple to be allowed to adopt a child."

"We could hardly believe it when we were granted the right to adopt him," chimed in Jacob. "Here is a picture taken the day it became official. Do you recognize anyone besides us?"

"That's Georgia," I answered, "although I almost didn't recognize her. You all have been friends for a long time."

"This picture was taken almost twenty years ago, and we had become friends a few years before that."

"What a cute picture," I said when we turned the page. It was one with Jacob, Peter, and Jeremy in a shallow pool spraying water on each other.

"Jeremy loved the water. One of the first things we did was enroll him in swimming lessons. As the years passed, we ended up in some fun water fights, either in the pool or chasing each other with the hose. Often, Jeremy was the instigator," Jacob said, and he showed a few other pictures of their antics with water. He then thumbed toward the middle of the album and pointed out another picture. "Here's a picture of him after winning a freestyle contest at a swim meet."

There were pictures of Jeremy graduating from middle school and dressed up for prom with a girl with a wide smile, and then a picture of Jeremy, Peter, and Jacob at his high school graduation.

"When it was time for graduation, Jeremy couldn't decide what he wanted to do next. He was pretty sure he wanted to eventually go into social work but didn't want to go right into college after high school. He decided he wanted to serve in the army, and then go to college afterwards," said Peter, emotion adding to his words, and he blinked away tears. "You can't believe how many times I ... we have wished he had chosen college first."

I gave him a hug without saying anything because I knew there were no words that could make up for the loss he and Jacob had been struggling with.

They turned to a picture of Jeremy in his uniform on his return from his basic training. He looked so happy, and another picture of the three of them showed how proud Jacob and Peter were of their handsome son.

The last picture in the album was of Jeremy after coming home from a third tour in Iraq. There was a change that was noticeable in his eyes and the seriousness of his demeanor. It was evident that he had lost his innocence about what was happening in the world.

"Two weeks after this picture was taken," Jacob said, "Jeremy drove to the Grand Canyon and jumped." His voice choked up as he said these words. "He had told us he was going fishing with a friend. We found the letter he wrote telling us about how he was feeling and that he couldn't deal with it anymore when we went to his apartment after his body was found."

"I feel so bad for both of you having gone through all of this. Thank you for sharing Jeremy's story with me. Now I can understand a little better your heartache."

"We count you as family, Casey, and felt like we wanted you to know what had happened," said Peter, and Jacob nodded in agreement. "Helping you through your challenges has really helped us too," added Peter.

"Yes," agreed Jacob. "We still have the heartache, and always will, but helping you has helped give us take our grief and use it to be of service rather than just sitting with it. I hope that makes some sense to you."

I nodded, and then I gave each one of them a hug. "As Georgia would probably say, if she were here, it's a God job."

Chapter 9

Staying with Jacob and Peter in their guest house had been the right transition for me after leaving the hospital, and I was grateful for that time of continued healing and support. I was grateful how our mutual sharing had brought closeness to our relationship. Now, though, it was time for me to move into my own home.

While I was still living with them, the three of us did a walkthrough with the house. Before the furniture was to be delivered, I wanted to truly make it mine.

Peter and I discussed color, texture, and what I thought I really wanted the home to represent and to be for me. When we had made the decisions and were ready to begin making the changes, Peter stepped in to help me paint the walls and to start decorating my new home. I loved the forest green focus wall and light turquoise walls with forest green, orange, and yellow accents. It was the perfect décor for a home close to the mountains and woods. It had all turned out prettier than any home I had of my own in the past. An electric fireplace had been installed, and when turned on, it glowed with a cheery fire.

Once I moved in, then Jacob and I started working to clean up the gardens and shrubbery outside. I tried to tell him I didn't have a green thumb, but he was having none of that. He was patient with me and made the work fun as he told stories and jokes. He explained to me about trimming, weeding, mulching, and all kinds of things I hadn't previously had experience with.

Jacob and I also had put in a container garden with herbs and vegetables and set up a drip system to water it. I had never had a garden with edible plants in it before, and I was looking forward to having vegetables I had grown. One of the changes I had made to help me in my recovery was to eat a plant-based diet, so having my own fresh, organic vegetables was important to me.

I was so grateful to all the work we had put into my home when it was finished.

When I looked in the mirror, I now saw someone shining with health. I had added ten most-needed pounds, my skin glowed, and I felt vibrant and alive for the first time in a long time. The depressed, anxious woman I had grown into because of neglecting myself was gone. Not only had I changed the way I was eating, but I now had exercise as a priority. I went running in the mornings, worked out at a gym three days a week, and had joined a yoga class. I looked like a new person, and I felt like it, too.

I saw a street sign one morning that I had noticed while out running, but really noticed it almost as if for the first time that day. I stopped and looked at it, and decided I would investigate further into it when I went home.

At home I opened my computer, and without checking emails, I searched for the website that had been displayed on the sign. When it popped up, I started reading and gathering information. I clicked on the button to find out about position openings and then filled out an application.

"Oh, my," I said to myself as I allowed the mouse to hover over the send button. I stopped, and took a deep breath. "Is this something I really want to do?" I went into the kitchen and made myself a cup of tea. As I sipped on the tea, I went back to the computer and looked at the application. "It isn't like I have to do this. I can do an interview with them, and if it isn't something I want to do, I don't have to do it." I sent the application. "I have no idea how long it will take to hear back from them." I chuckled at my trepidation and then congratulated myself on being willing to take an action step.

I knew in my heart I had been given a new life, and now it was time for me to give back.

About ten o'clock I was putting groceries away when my phone rang.

"Hello, I'm Diana, from Hospice of the Pines, calling for Casey Granger."

"This is Casey."

"I am the director of volunteers, and I'm calling because we received your application this morning, and I wanted to say thank you. We would like you to come in for an interview and talk more about our program. How did you hear about us?"

I chuckled. "I was out running this morning and saw your billboard. I know I've seen it before, but for some reason, this morning it practically stopped me in my tracks. My husband died in hospice a little over a year ago, and I've been thinking it is now time for me to give back for all of the support I have received. Seeing your sign seemed like it might be something I could do."

"It's been over a year," she said thoughtfully. "We take that into consideration with people, because if it is too soon after a death has occurred, it can be challenging to work with people who are dying. You said you have been getting support, and I'm glad to hear it. I would enjoy talking to you more, and seeing what you think, Casey."

We set a time for the two of us to meet the next afternoon. I was looking forward to meeting her in person and to hear more about what volunteering with them might look like.

As I walked in through the double glass doors, I was greeted by a smiling young man with a radio talk show voice. "Hi, welcome to Hospice of the Pines. How may I help you?"

"I'm looking for the volunteer department. My name is Casey Granger, and I have an appointment."

"Let me give Diana a call to let her know you are here." The words were barely out of his mouth when a woman with blond hair and dark brown eyes came around the corner. "Well, never mind. Diana," he said, laughing, "I had my finger on the phone ready to call you. This is Casey Granger."

"Hello, Casey," Diana said. "Thank you, Steve," she said to the young man who had greeted me. "Steve is the voice of Hospice of the Pines. I believe some people just call in to hear his voice."

"But of course, Diana. The reason they decide to do business with us is because I have charmed them."

"Be careful, Casey, or he will have you drawn into his web. Oh no, what have I done?" Diana said, laughing. "You have a big enough head already without me adding more."

I enjoyed listening to their friendly banter. Instead of feeling like an outsider, I felt included in it.

We went to Diana's office, after making a quick stop in the break room for a bottle of water for me, and for Diana to refill her coffee cup. Her office was a welcoming room with pictures of Diana's family, and some pictures of staff and volunteers gathered for different occasions.

Diana interviewed me about my past experiences with death.

"It has been a little over a year since my husband died. I was grateful to have hospice come in to help make him more comfortable and to give me support."

"Sometimes working with people who are dying can trigger our own experiences we have had with our own family," replied Diana. "We are here to support you if this happens for you. Do you have resources to help you outside of hospice?"

"Yes, I do," I reassured her. "I have been seeing a therapist, and I have some wonderful friends who have been there to support me. I believe I can use my past experiences to support others going through similar things."

We talked about the training each volunteer was required to take before being allowed to volunteer. It would be one day a week for six weeks. They wanted to make sure the volunteers were comfortable with working with clients at the end of life, their families, and their caregivers. Hospice also wanted the volunteers to completely understand their role and how important it was. The training was beginning in two weeks.

"So, what do you think, Casey? Would you like some time to think about all of this before making a decision?"

I shook my head. "I believe this is something I would like to do."

Diana gave me a quick hug. "I'm so glad."

Before I left, Diana gave me a tour of their facility, introduced me to some of the people we saw, and arranged for me to do a ride-along with one of their chaplains the following week so I could see firsthand what it was all about. I would still be able to opt out of my decision if, after riding with the chaplain, I had second thoughts. Diana had also given me the dates for the training and her card in case any questions came up for me after I left.

Tuesday of the following week, I was back at Hospice of the Pines. I greeted Steve and let him know I was there to meet Chaplain Dave Garcia.

It didn't take long before a man came and greeted me. "Hello, Mrs. Granger. It's nice to meet you. I'm Dave Garcia. I hear that I have the pleasure of your company this morning." Dave Garcia was over six feet tall, with dark, curling hair, smooth dark skin, and sparkling amber eyes. His smile was infectious. At five-foot-four, I felt like a dwarf next to this gentle giant, as my hand was lost in his hand. He was wearing a dark olive shirt with a collar like a priest.

"It's nice to meet you, too, Rev. Dave. Please call me Casey. Mrs. Granger was my mother-in-law."

"And I go by Dave. We aren't very formal around here. I have our schedule figured out, and we can leave if you are ready. By the way, if you feel like after a couple of visits you would like to stop, just let me know, and I will bring you back here."

"Thank you. I'm looking forward to being with you this morning."

After spending the time with Chaplain Dave, I was convinced that volunteering with hospice was something I really wanted to do. I enjoyed his calm, easy way of being with both the patients and their family members. It convinced me this was a way I could contribute to others. After being looked after by others for so many months, I realized I wanted to find a way to serve people.

***

"I am so excited," I said as I assembled place settings on my table.

It looked fun and festive. I placed a rolled cloth napkin on each plate, and on top of the napkin was a bright-colored noisemaker like people use on New Year's Eve. I was getting ready for my first house party since moving into my little home two months before. I was now ready to celebrate all that had happened. Georgia had asked about bringing someone with her, so I had added an extra place setting. I had not yet met the man she was dating, but I was glad she was going to bring him with her.

This was to be a celebration, and an opportunity for me to show my gratitude to my Three Musketeers who had been in my corner cheering me on each step of the way.

I made a quick pass through my home to see if there was anything I needed to do. Then I went to change into a dress Georgia and I had found when we went shopping at a new boutique. It was fun, sleeveless, with a swishy skirt and bright blue and orange flowers. I slipped my feet into navy sandals with a wedge heel and did a turn in front of the mirror with a big smile on my face.

I had seen a framed affirmation that seemed to fit the way I felt now. It said, "Every day, in every way, everything is getting better and better." I had purchased it knowing it was true for me.

I heard the doorbell ring a few minutes later and smiled. My guests had started to arrive. "Jacob and Peter, it's so good to see you," I said, giving each of them a warm hug.

"Everything looks so nice," Peter said. "I like what you've done with the place."

"Of course, you do, since you helped me put it all together."

"I helped you," he said. Then with a quick shake of his head, he added, "But you are the one who ultimately made the decisions. We made a good team."

"We did, and it was a lot of fun."

A few minutes later there was a brief knock at the door, and Georgia came through the open door. A familiar man was at her side.

"Dave! I wasn't expecting to see you so soon," I exclaimed as I recognized Dave Garcia, the chaplain I had been riding with on Tuesday. I came forward and gave him a hug and then hugged Georgia.

"I would say I don't have to introduce the two of you," said Georgia smiling. "I didn't realize you knew Casey, Dave. By the way, Peter and Jacob, this is Dave. Dave, these are my other friends I wanted you to meet, Peter and Jacob."

"I met Casey at Hospice of the Pines earlier this week," Dave said as he returned my hug. "She went on a ride-along with me to see what it might be like for her as a volunteer." Then he shook hands with Peter and Jacob.

Three pairs of eyes turned toward me, and everyone started talking at once, and then we started laughing.

"I'm excited for you, Casey," said Georgia. "I had no idea you were thinking about going to work as a volunteer. This must be one of the answers to your what's next question, it sounds like."

I nodded. "I have had so much love and support over the last months, and I decided it was time for me to give back." I further explained how I had seen the sign while out running and then called the number.

"Something smells good, Casey. What can we do to help?" asked Jacob as we started moving toward the kitchen.

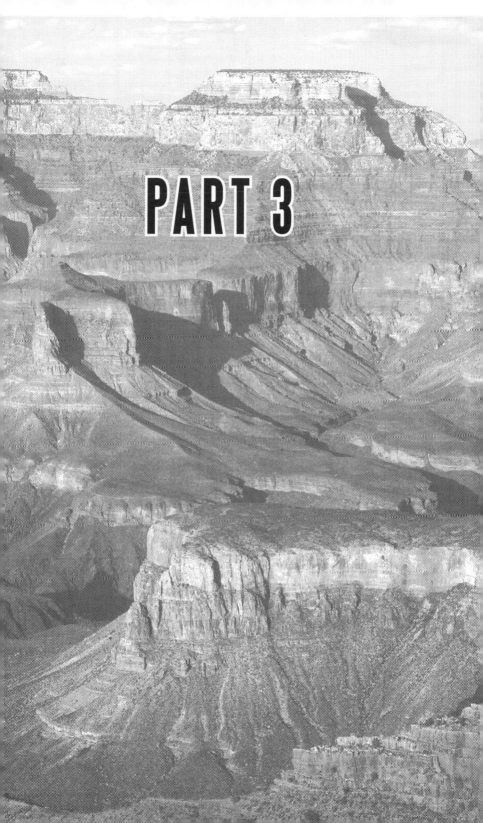

PART 3

Chapter 10

Since moving into my home, I hadn't noticed anyone at the house next door. There had been gardeners a couple of times but not any noticeable activity other than them. I wondered if the house was empty, but I would shrug my shoulders, not curious enough to do anything more than wonder. So I was surprised when I saw a slender young man with short, shaggy hair and glasses come down from the porch with a bicycle. He waved at me, a friendly grin spreading on his face.

"You must be the new lady who just moved in a few months ago. I'm Greg. This is my grandfather's home."

"Yes, I'm the new lady. My name is Casey. It's nice to meet you. I wasn't sure anyone lived there. Other than gardeners, I haven't seen anyone until you." I laughed. "Boy, does that make me sound like the neighborhood snoop."

Greg laughed with me. "I would think you were odd if you didn't have some curiosity about the people who live near you. My grandfather has been gone all summer helping to build some schools. I've been here every week since I returned from working with him, to check on things, but haven't seen you either. Grandpa is coming home in a couple of days, and then you will get to see who lives here. I've got to get going," Greg said as he climbed on his bike. "It was nice meeting you, Casey."

"Same here, Greg."

I watched Greg head down the street and then laughed at myself. "Now my curiosity is really piqued after talking to Greg. I had better watch out if I don't want to actually become the neighborhood snoop."

***

On Saturday I came home after my last class to become a hospice volunteer feeling proud at this completion, grateful it was done, and a little sad that I would only be seeing my fellow volunteers sporadically until our quarterly meetings, when we would join other volunteers. I decided to go in and change into something more comfortable for a quiet evening at home, but when I went into my bedroom, I could hear the sound of water running at the side of the house.

I hurried out without even changing out of the pumps I was wearing on my feet, and saw water pouring from a valve on the side of my neighbor's house and spewing into my yard. Quickly I ran up the slight embankment to the cause of the flood, and I put my hand on the handle, starting to tighten it when the handle came off in my hand.

"What are you doing?" an angry voice said, and I was not too gently moved out of the way.

"What does it look like I'm doing?" I shouted back at the man in front of me. "This thing was pouring water into my yard, and I was trying to shut it off!"

"Well it doesn't look like you succeeded, and now things are worse. I've got to go in and turn the water off. Don't do anything else!"

I glared at the bully. "Don't worry, I won't!" I started to leave and slipped in the muddy earth under my feet and started to fall. He reached out and grabbed my arm. "Don't touch me. Leave me alone," I said, shaking off his hand. I started to step away, and I slipped again and ended up landing on my butt before he could catch me again. The water was now pouring down on me. He pulled me to my feet.

"Are you all right?" he said. "Did you hurt yourself?"

"Am I all right? You've got to be kidding! Do I look all right?" I said slowly and I glared at him like he was an imbecile for even asking. I shook his hands off me, and glaring at him one more time, I carefully made my way back into my own yard, with my feet squishing with every step in my soaked and muddied shoes.

He started to speak, and I ignored him. I was starting to shiver in my thoroughly wet clothes, and all I wanted to do was get away from him.

When I was back in my yard, I looked back, but the man was not there. Apparently he had left to turn off the water because there was no longer water gushing out from his yard into mine.

"I guess I just met Grandpa," I muttered to myself. I started to go into the house through the French doors leading into my kitchen, and I realized I would be making a mess.

I was reaching in to turn off the patio lights when Grandpa came hurrying up from behind me with towels in his hands. "Let me help you," he said. He noticed I was shivering. "Let's get you dried off and out of those wet clothes. It's the least I can do. I apologize for coming on to you like you were the one at fault." He started putting actions to his words, and I stopped him.

"Believe it or not, I can take care of this myself. All I want to do is get out of these clothes, and I can't do that with you standing here. You've done your good deed. Now please leave. I don't want your help."

He looked at me for a moment. "Okay. I do want to let you know I feel bad about this."

I watched him leave and suddenly felt alone.

***

After a warm shower, and getting dressed in some soft, casual slacks and a light sweater, I felt better. I went into the laundry room where I had taken off my clothes, and I put them in the deep sink to rinse them off and remove the mud. My shoes were ruined, and I threw them in the trash.

"Not quite the evening I had planned. I'm glad the shoes weren't handmade Italian," I said with a laugh.

I went into the kitchen and took out a container of soup I had made that morning. When I had made the soup, I had been thinking about how the weather was turning cooler and how it would be a welcome addition to the evening. Now, after being soaking wet in those cooler temperatures, I knew it would be just what the doctor ordered.

After turning on the electric fireplace, I ladled some of the now-heated soup into a bowl. I carried it into the living room and curled up in my favorite chair. I almost spilled the soup on myself when a firm knock sounded on the front door.

I looked out one of the front windows and briefly thought about ignoring the visitor standing on my porch.

"Hello," I said as I opened the door. "How may I help you?"

"I want to apologize for what happened earlier. I was angry at myself and frustrated, and I took it out on you." He handed me a bouquet of pretty fall flowers. "I hope you will accept these as a token of my apologies. I don't usually greet my neighbors the way I did you. My name is Simon Williams."

I took the flowers, and he started to turn away. "Thank you," I said, and I lifted the bouquet up to my nose, where I could breathe in their fragrance. "They are beautiful. I'm Casey Granger."

"I better get back to my project so I can get the water turned back on. I'm glad you like the flowers. I wasn't sure you would open the door, much less accept my peace offering."

I laughed. "When I saw you standing out here I wasn't sure I wanted to open the door, but I'm glad I did. Fresh flowers are always a nice addition to my home, and I'm grateful we won't feel like we have to continue to glare when we see each other. I trust everything goes well with your project."

Simon looked at me for a few moments, his deep green eyes thoughtful. "Thanks." He turned away, and I watched him until he disappeared into his own home.

"Wow! I didn't expect that after our run-in earlier, but I'm glad he came over. I wouldn't want to be carrying on some kind of feud with him. It isn't my style, and it would change the whole dynamics of the neighborhood for me. Fortunately, it seems he felt similarly." Once again, I lifted the flowers up to my nose and smiled. "I better put you guys in some water."

After I placed the flowers in an earthenware vase and found a home for them on the dining room table, I went back to my forgotten soup I had left in the living room. It had grown cool, so I placed it in the microwave to reheat, and my mind returned to my surprise visitor.

He had been wearing a green and yellow plaid flannel shirt with the sleeves rolled up to the elbow that seemed to intensify the green of his eyes. His silver-gray hair was cut short in a no-nonsense military style. With his broad shoulders and large hands, he had the look of someone who spent little time behind a desk. Then I remembered his grandson, Greg, telling me that Simon had been gone all summer building schools.

I took my soup back into the living room and settled into my comfortable chair. The soup was hot, so I put it down and picked up the book I had been reading, but I had a hard time concentrating on it.

Chapter 11

Two days later I received a phone call from Diana at Hospice of the Pines. "Hi, Casey. I have a patient who would like to have a volunteer. She is forty-five years old and has cancer. She's been on service for a couple of months, and she has now decided she would like to have a volunteer. Do you feel like you're ready to volunteer?"

"I would love to, Diana. I'm so glad you offered."

"Great! I will give your name to the social worker, Edna, and she will give you a call. After you speak to Edna, you can decide if this will be a fit for you. Then, if it is, I will have a sheet with the patient's information on it for you here in the office. Thank you so much for considering it."

"You're welcome. I'm looking forward to it, Diana."

An hour later, Edna called, and we arranged for the two of us to meet and speak in person about the patient. I invited her to come to my home, and she accepted.

"Hi, Casey? I'm Edna," the woman on my porch said. Her sparkling hazel eyes were shining as I opened the door. She shifted her briefcase to her other hand and offered her right hand to shake my hand.

"It's nice to meet you, Edna. I have fresh coffee if you would like some."

"That sounds great."

We sat down at the dining room table, and Edna took a paper out of her briefcase. "I spoke to Diana before coming here to let her know we were meeting, and she gave me your paperwork for Emily. Let me tell you a little about her, so you can get a picture of what is happening with her."

I nodded and Edna continued. "Emily has been through almost every kind of treatment that could be thought of for her cancer. She made the decision to stop, and her husband has been bitter about it. His name is Joe. He works from home and has been her main caregiver. He was unwilling for her to come onto hospice in the first place, and he was the main holdout when it came to Emily having a volunteer. He admits that her being placed on hospice robbed him of any sense of hope and that having people come into help her with her pills, to bathe her, and to be available for her emotional support was like saying he had failed to do what he had been doing for her. He thought we were coming in thinking we could do things better than he had. Joe didn't understand we were there to support him also. There are no children, and their extended family do not live in the area."

"I can see why you wanted to talk with me about her before I made a decision to be her volunteer, Edna. How is her husband doing now that she has been on service for a while?"

"He is accepting us better and is finally seeing we are there to support both of them. He hasn't been leaving the house to do things except for a quick run to the store, and now he's having groceries delivered, so he isn't even doing that. I'm hoping with you coming in, he will feel like he can leave for a few hours to do things for himself."

"I went through similar things with my husband before he died, so I can somewhat understand where he's coming from," I said. "I believe I could be of support to them."

"I'm glad to hear it," said Edna, and she handed me the paperwork she had brought for me. "All of her information you will need is here, and the nursing care plan for a volunteer. Linda is her case manager, and if you have any questions when you visit Emily, you can call Linda or myself. I know you learned this in your volunteer training, and so I am only reminding you, that we work as a team, and now you are a part of the team. Do you have any thoughts or questions for me?"

"I'm feeling excited and a little scared at the same time. I wouldn't want to say or do anything that would be a detriment to Emily or her husband."

"Diana sang your praises to me when I was talking to her about the case, and she has no doubts about your ability. She is a huge resource for you. It's natural to have some doubts when you start out, Casey, because being a volunteer is new to you. Once you get your feet wet, you will be fine, and you will laugh about the feelings you had when you started. Anything else?"

"I can't think of anything else right now. Thank you so much for coming over to meet with me, Edna. I really appreciate it."

"Now, I have a face to go with the name, and I like that. If you have any questions after I leave or after you speak with Emily, give me a call or a text," Edna said as she picked up her briefcase and prepared to leave. She gave me a hug. "Thank you for the coffee. It was nice to meet you."

"You are very welcome. I'm glad to be joining your team."

I remembered a few words of a prayer as I sat down to make the phone call to Emily. "Lord, make me an instrument of Thy peace." I closed my eyes for a moment and contemplated those words.

"Good morning," I said as a male voice answered. "This is Casey Granger. I'm a volunteer with Hospice of the Pines."

"Yeah, Edna said you would be calling. When will you be coming to see Emily?"

"I would like to come today, if it's convenient for you, or tomorrow."

"Yeah, today works. What time?"

I took a deep breath to center myself. I hadn't realized I had been holding my breath. It was challenging for me to not respond in kind to this man's coldness. "How about one p.m.?"

"That'll be good. It's right after she eats. Much later than that and she would probably be asleep."

Half an hour later I received a call from Diana at Hospice of the Pines. "Hi, Casey. The spouse of Emily just called and asked if you could come tomorrow instead. The nurse's aide called, apparently right after you did. She was asking to come at the time you were coming. He doesn't want to overexert her with too many people."

"That's fine. I will give him a call back and set up a time for tomorrow."

"Thanks for accepting this family, Casey. He seems to be really hurting, and I know having someone coming into help give him some time to take care of some of his own needs may be really helpful."

"You're welcome. My having had a similar experience to his may help me have more empathy for him."

***

At ten the next morning, I took a deep breath as I locked my car I had parked in front of Emily and Joe's home. We had arranged for my visit with Emily to be after Emily's breakfast time, when she seemed to have more energy. I had decided to allow Joe to make decisions about how I could best be of service to them. I was willing to go with the flow of what it would all look like rather than having my own agenda.

A man stepped through the front door. His hair was shaggy, and he had a couple days' growth of beard on his face. He wore faded jeans and a T-shirt, and his feet were bare. "You must be Casey," he said. "I'm Joe." There was no warmth in his voice.

"It's good to meet you, Joe."

He turned, and I followed him into the kitchen area, where breakfast dishes were sitting next to the sink, and it looked like the previous evening's dishes were in the sink.

"It's a mess," he said, flushing slightly, his voice gruff and defensive. "I was tired last evening, and didn't get things done. We didn't have a good day yesterday."

I said gently, "You have a lot on your plate, and I'm grateful to be here. I hope my visits will help you."

"I was thinking about that, and what you could do for me—for us. Why don't you stay with Emily while I go out to get some groceries? The big thing is not to wear her out. She tires really easy.

"That sounds like a good plan to me."

I followed him into the master bedroom, keeping my attention on him rather than on the chair filled with what looked like laundry that had been dumped there after being laundered, and another chair with unopened mail and newspapers. It was obvious that housekeeping had taken a backseat to the other priorities of caring for someone who was very ill. I knew from firsthand experience what that looked like, even though my own situation had been different.

The woman lying in the bed had her eyes closed when we first entered the room. Her hair was sparse as a result of chemotherapy, her skin was pale, and her body was emaciated. She looked like a refugee from a concentration camp with her hollow cheeks and rounded belly.

Joe spoke to her softly. "Em." Her eyes fluttered open, blank at first, and then she focused as he continued speaking. "The lady from hospice is here that I told you about."

A smile slowly brightened her face, and her dull eyes seemed to come alive. "You caught me napping," she said. "It's one of the best things I do as of late," she said with a chuckle. "I'm Emily."

I went closer to her and gently took the hand she was holding out. "Hi, Emily, my name is Casey. I'm glad to meet you, and I'm grateful to both you and Joe allowing me to come into your home."

"Em, I'm going to do some grocery shopping, and she's going to stay here with you while I'm gone."

"That sounds like a great idea, but why don't you take a nap first, honey? You look like some sleep is what the doctor ordered. Then you will feel more like shopping, which isn't your favorite thing to do anyway."

He started to protest that I may not want to stay that long, and Emily looked toward me.

"It's not a problem for me," I said.

Emily smiled her thanks and continued. "Joe, while you're out, why don't you get a haircut? Otherwise we are going to have to dig out my old rollers and curl your hair," Emily teased him with a gentle smile on her face and love that radiated from her eyes.

"Yeah, like that's going to happen," he said, returning her banter, and reached down to give her a kiss. "I will just be in the guest room if either of you need anything," Joe added as he turned away from her.

A few moments later I heard a door down the hallway close, and I watched as Emily's bright blue eyes filled with tears. I knelt next to her bed and held her hand. She cried quietly for a few moments and then swiped at her tears with her other hand. I handed her a tissue, and she wiped her eyes and blew her nose.

Her voice was rough when she spoke. "This has been so hard on Joe. We don't have any close family, so he's had the burden of caring for me and trying to keep his business going at the same time."

I nodded but didn't say anything, and Emily continued to speak, "We couldn't have children, and I had finally convinced him that we ought to try to adopt a child when I was diagnosed with cancer. That stopped all of our plans, and it has changed everything."

I continued to hold her hand quietly until the tears stopped, and she looked at me with a rueful grin, "Sorry, I don't usually dump on someone five minutes after meeting them."

I patted her hand and replied, "Emily, I'm grateful you felt like you could trust me enough to share what has been going on with you. Is there anything I can do for you?"

"Actually, you could. I'm really tired of being in this bed. If you can move my walker over here, I would like to move over to that recliner chair. It takes me a few minutes, I move like a turtle, but with you here and using my walker, I can get over there."

I offered my hand for Emily to move to a sitting position with her legs hanging over the side of the bed. She sat there for a couple of minutes, and then I brought her walker over close to her.

The whole process was slow, and Emily was exhausted once she was seated in the recliner with pillows supporting her and a quilted afghan covering her stomach and legs. She relaxed into the chair and closed her eyes. "It takes a lot of effort, but it is so worth it. Sometimes I feel imprisoned when I'm in bed. When I'm up in this chair, I can look out and experience some of mother nature."

"Would you like some water or something, Emily?"

"That would be great. Thank you. Joe keeps a pitcher of lemon water in the fridge for me. You could get some for yourself too if you would like some."

I returned a few minutes later with two glasses of water. We talked some, and Emily dozed off. I picked up a nearby magazine and paged through it, looking at some of the pictures and reading a few of the articles.

It had been a little over an hour when Joe stuck his head in the door. He frowned when he saw Emily sleeping in the chair. "I usually carry her over there."

"She asked me to help her, and I hope that was okay. She said she was tired of being in bed."

"I should have gotten her up before you came, but I didn't think about it. I'm going to take a quick shower and then go do the shopping. Do you need anything?"

"No, I'm fine."

Before he left to go shopping, Joe showed me some prefilled syringes. "If she starts feeling pain, you can hand her one of these," he said, "and this is my cell number if you need anything. She probably ought to just stay in the chair, and I will help her back to bed when I come home."

"Here is my card if you feel like you want to check to see how she is doing," I said. "I have my cell phone number on the back of it."

Right after Joe left, Emily woke up. "Sorry, I didn't mean to conk out on you," she said with a yawn.

"No problem. Walking over from the bed really tuckered you out." I explained to her that Joe had just left, and she nodded.

"I'm glad he is getting out of the house, even for just a little while. He's been trapped in here with me for a while now. He started having groceries delivered, and it's been ages since he went for a haircut or did anything for himself. I feel kind of hungry. There is some pudding in the frig. Would you mind getting some for me?"

"I would be glad to, Emily."

When Joe returned about an hour later with a fresh haircut, Emily was awake and greeted him enthusiastically. "There's my man! You look good enough to eat."

"Wow! It sounds like you are getting your appetite back if I look like food." He turned to me. "Thanks for staying with her."

"You are welcome."

We set up a time and date for me to come back at the end of the week for a couple of hours, and then I left. It felt so good to know I had been able to help them. I now knew my decision to volunteer with hospice had been the right choice for me.

When I arrived home a little while later, I received a call from Emily's social worker, Edna. "I just had a phone call with Joe," she said.

"Oh, is everything all right?"

"Yes. He wanted to let me know that having you come was a good idea, and it helped more than he thought it would. I'm glad you decided to be their volunteer, Casey."

"Thank you for calling me, Edna. I didn't quite know what to expect. I was afraid you were calling to say Joe was upset about something."

"No, he didn't say anything like that. It may take time for him to warm up to you. He has been doing everything for her for so long that he doesn't seem to trust easily. He was the same way with me, and with the nurse, when we started. Try not to let his attitude discourage you."

"I can understand where he's coming from, and I'm grateful for the opportunity to support them."

***

The next time I went to see Emily and Joe, Emily was already sitting in the recliner in their bedroom. "I'm so glad to see you, Casey. Did Joe tell you he and an old friend of his are going to meet for coffee? I would be willing to bet it has been almost a year, or longer, since Joe has been willing to leave me that long for something he wanted to do."

"That makes me happy and grateful to be coming to spend time with you," I replied, and I gave her a hug. "Is there anything you would like me to help you with while I'm here today?"

Emily nodded, and her eyes misted over with tears. "I've been wanting to write some letters to people in my life to let them know how much they have meant to me and how I am feeling. They are kind of goodbye letters. I haven't mentioned it to Joe, because I know it would be hard on him, and besides, one of the letters would be to him." She swiped at her eyes before continuing. "I will write as much as I can of the letter to Joe. Writing really tires me out, though, so I would appreciate it if you would write the other letters. We can let those people know you are writing for me, and then I will sign them, and maybe add a note to them myself."

"What a beautiful idea, Emily. I am glad to be able to help you with the letters."

She told me where to find the writing materials, and I found some lovely lavender-colored stationary with her initials embossed at the top.

"Joe gave me the stationary for my birthday, because he knows how much I enjoy writing letters. These are the first letters I have written in several months."

While Emily started on the letter to Joe, I went into the kitchen to make each of us a cup of tea. I could tell Joe seemed to be doing a little better because the kitchen was clean, and there were other areas that were less cluttered than on my previous visit.

When I returned to the bedroom, Emily was resting with her head laid back against the recliner, her eyes closed. She opened her eyes when I entered the room. "This is harder than I thought," she said, pointing to the letter she had started to Joe. "Not physically, but emotionally. I realize he will be reading it when I am gone, and I won't physically be here to show him my love. He is such a great guy and has been so supportive of me."

"You are very brave and thoughtful to have the desire to do this for Joe and the other people who mean a lot to you."

"Thank you, Casey, and thank you for the tea."

Emily completed the letter to Joe, and after sealing it in an envelope, we started writing the other letters. We had just completed them and put them in a safe place when Joe returned.

"There's my girl," he said, coming into the room. "How you doing, Em?"

"I'm doing good. Casey and I have had a good visit. How was your time with Tom?"

"I enjoyed it, and I'm sure he did, too."

***

I called Georgia as I was walking to my car from Emily and Joe's home. "Hi, I was wondering if you have had lunch yet, and if you are able to meet me?"

"I love your spontaneity, Casey, and I had just started thinking that it must be time for lunch."

We decided on a cozy café where we had shared meals before. I loved the hominess of the atmosphere, and on this cool fall day, I was grateful for the crackling fireplace the tables surrounded.

Georgia arrived a few minutes after I did, and after giving our order to the waiter, Georgia commented, "I'm so glad you called. We've been having meetings all morning, and I was ready to get away for a little while. I was going to go home and heat up some leftovers. This is a lot more fun than that."

"I'm glad you could meet, too. You can always have the leftovers tonight."

She nodded. "Maybe, but I hate to feed Dave the same thing we had last night," she said, and laughed.

"Oh yeah." I chuckled. "It might run him off if he has to eat the same thing two nights in a row. He is a nice guy, though, and he probably wouldn't complain. I'm sure he realizes how special you are."

"You are probably right. So, what's up with you? I noticed something in your voice when you called."

"I was just leaving the home of the couple I am volunteering for when I called you. My visit with her was pretty emotional, and I wanted someone I could be myself with for a while." I went on to explain about the letters Emily wanted us to write.

Georgia dabbed at her eyes with her napkin. "What a special thing for her to want to do. I'm glad you were able to help her. Did all of this trigger things for you that you went through with Richard?"

"In a way, I guess. It wasn't about not receiving letters for sure, because Richard had never been a letter writer, and more often than not, he would give me money or gift cards as gifts.

He didn't think anything he could think to buy me would be something I would want." I shrugged, and then I continued. "What triggered me was the love she expressed in the letters and the love that emanates from them when they are together. Richard and I hadn't been that way for a long time."

Georgia reached over and squeezed my hand. She waited to speak until the waiter served us our meal and brought more coffee. "I hear you, Casey. I can understand why this was hard on you. Thank you for sharing your experience with me.

"What may help you to think about is that you and Richard were married for a much longer time than this young couple, and Richard's diagnosis was different. From what you have shared with me in the past, you and Richard had a very loving relationship before your mother became ill and needed more of your care.

"It hurts you when you compare your marriage to theirs. Comparisons often have us seeing ourselves more negatively than the person we are comparing ourselves to. I would suggest that a better focus would be to remember the good times you and Richard had, and to appreciate how you were there for him and took care of him. Does that make sense?"

I thought about her words for a moment and then nodded. "Thank you, Georgia. You are so wise. I knew you were the right person for me to talk to about this."

"I admire you for being there for this couple, Casey. I know you are making a difference."

I loved being with Georgia and was grateful I had called her. Before the luncheon was over, we were talking and laughing. She also shared with me about plans she and Dave had for the following weekend, and I was happy for her.

I was putting on my jacket preparing to leave the restaurant when I noticed a familiar silver-haired man come through the door. His eyes lighted on me for a moment as he greeted the waiter, and then his gaze returned to me, and he came over to our table.

"Mrs. Granger, I almost didn't recognize you," he said with his deep voice.

"Please call me Casey. Georgia, I would like you to meet my neighbor, Simon Williams. Mr. Williams, this is my good friend Georgia Smith."

"It's Simon," he said simply as he acknowledged Georgia. Georgia's small hand was lost in Simon's larger hand as they shook hands.

"Nice to meet you, Simon." Georgia glanced at her watch. "It's time for me to get back to work. I will talk to you later, Casey." She and I hugged each other before Georgia left.

"It was nice seeing you, Simon. I hope you enjoy your lunch."

"I'm sure I will. I'm glad our bumping into each other this time wasn't quite so traumatic."

"Me too," I agreed, smiling.

"Um, would you consider going out for dinner with me sometime?"

"I think I would like that, Simon, as long as there are no waterworks involved." I took one of my cards out of my purse. "Here's my number. You can give me a call, or I guess you could knock on the door."

"Thanks," he said, and his smile reached his green eyes as he acknowledged my teasing. "I will do my best to keep gushing water out of it."

I couldn't help smiling as I left the restaurant a few minutes later. I didn't have to look back to know that Simon was watching me.

***

The next time I visited Emily, she was in bed sleeping. "She's been sleeping a lot lately," said Joe in a whisper, "they tell me it's part of the process." He choked up. "She's getting ready to leave me."

There was nothing I could really say, but I was glad he felt like he could share it with me and that he trusted me with his vulnerability. I put an arm around him.

"I don't know if I should go anywhere today," he said. "I know they have told me she may leave some time when I just step out of the room, but I don't think I could bear it if she decided to leave when I was out of the house. What do you think I should do, Casey?"

"Is there something you could do for yourself without going somewhere, Joe? Maybe reading or taking a nap or working in the yard, or whatever would be something that would help you."

He thought about it for a minute. "Yes, those are good ideas. I think getting out and working in the yard would help me a lot. I've always enjoyed working with plants and being outdoors, although, looking at our yard right now, you wouldn't know it."

"I think you have had a few other priorities to handle rather than the yard," I said gently. "If that's what you would like to do, I can sit in here with Emily. I brought a book to read. I will let you know if there is any change."

"Thank you. I'm glad you are here."

A little while later I heard Joe whistling as he went out into the cool fall day, and I smiled. I had just retrieved my book from my bag when Emily opened her eyes groggily. At first her eyes were unfocused, and a slight frown appeared on her forehead. I went over to her and gently patted her hand.

"Good morning, Emily," I said gently.

Gradually her eyes focused on me, and her mouth curved in a smile. "Hi, Casey. I guess you caught me sleeping," she said slowly.

"I did. Is there anything I can get for you?"

Emily shook her head. "No. Sorry to be such a bore, but I think I just want to rest for a little while." She closed her eyes again, and I could tell from her breathing that she had returned to sleep.

Joe worked out in the yard for a couple of hours, taking a couple of breaks to peek in to see how Emily was doing, and then returning to his work. He smiled easily, his cheeks were rosy from the cooler temperatures, and his eyes were sparkling. It was easy for Casey to see that getting outdoors and doing the yardwork were helping to revive his spirits.

When I left a while later, I felt sad as I noticed the changes happening with Emily. At the same time, I was grateful I had been there so that Joe had felt comfortable in being outdoors and able to care for himself.

Chapter 12

It was raining when I woke up. I looked out the window, and the sky was overcast. I looked at the clock at the bedside, and it said six, but because it was overcast, it felt like it was earlier than that. I was tempted to stay under the covers and hibernate.

My phone rang, and I wondered who would be calling so early in the day. I looked at the caller ID and answered it.

"Casey, she's gone," Joe sobbed. "I have been up all night with her, and she looked up at me, and then she stopped breathing. I don't know what to do."

"Joe, have you called hospice? They will send someone over to help support you."

"No, I haven't called them. You are right. Thank you for reminding me. They all told me to call them when it happened, but I just couldn't think about what I was supposed to do."

"I can understand, Joe. Give them a call, and they will come and help you take care of things. I'm sorry, Joe, for what you are going through."

A few minutes later when the call was ended, I sat on the edge of the bed, looking at the phone I still held in my hand. Tears started trekking down my cheeks, and I grabbed a tissue. I knew Emily's condition had changed, but I hadn't realized she was so close to dying. I felt sad for Joe, and I also felt sad for myself that I had not had a lot of time with her.

I looked out at the rain. "It is perfect that it is raining," I said. "It's like the universe is grieving, too."

Now it was really tempting just to go back to bed, but I didn't. I put on my robe and slippers and went into the kitchen. The preset timer on the coffee had worked, and so fresh coffee was waiting for me. I poured a cup, and cup in hand, I went into the living room and turned on the fireplace, grateful for the warmth and the welcoming glow.

Today I would have been going to visit with Emily, so now I would be doing things differently than I had planned.

Instead of jumping into planning mode, though, I sipped on my coffee and thought about Joe and Emily. I rubbed the center of my chest gently, where I could feel the ache of sadness for a life seemingly too short, and for the grief Joe would be having to deal with now. Tears trickled unheeded down my cheeks. I sat for a while with those feelings, realizing I needed to allow the feelings to be expressed rather than stuffing them down inside of me like I had in the past. I knew by taking care of myself in this way that I would be able to better deal with Emily's passing and be able to continue to volunteer with other families in similar situations. I was grateful to have this realization of what would best serve me in the long run.

I wasn't sure how long I sat there. My coffee cup was empty, but I hadn't wanted to interrupt what was happening with me to retrieve more. The phone rang, and I looked at the caller ID.

"Hello, Casey. I hope I didn't awaken you. This is Diana from Hospice of the Pines."

"No, you didn't wake me up, Diana. I've been up for quite some time."

"That's good. I wanted to give you the news that the patient you have been volunteering for died this morning."

"I appreciate you calling me. Her husband called me right after it happened. He had forgotten what he was supposed to do when she died, and so he called me. I was able to let him know to call hospice and they would send people to support him."

"I'm glad you were able to help him. It's not unusual under the circumstances for people to forget to call us. Sometimes, instead, they call the police, and that only complicates things. How are you doing, Casey? I know they were the first family you volunteered with, and I want to let you know I'm here for you if you need someone to talk about it with."

"Thank you. I will remember if I feel like I need to. Actually, I have been taking some time this morning to work through my feelings about it. My therapist would be proud of me. I know it's important for me to deal with my own feelings in order for me to continue to work as a hospice volunteer, and besides, stuffing my feelings would only hurt me in the long run. I'm learning from the way I used to do things."

"Good for you. I am grateful to have you on our team, Casey. Give yourself whatever time you need, and when you are ready for a new family, let me know."

"I will do that. Thank you so much for calling me. I will be in touch soon, Diana."

I looked outside at the rain continuing to fall after my phone call with Diana. I was grateful to be part of a loving team that wanted to make sure I was informed. It certainly had not always been the way things were when I worked in my previous nursing career.

"It looks like this is a good day to work around the house," I said to myself. "I was going to do it tomorrow, but staying inside seems like a good idea."

The phone rang late in the morning. I was finished with cleaning and had just stepped out of the shower.

"Good morning. This is Simon, from next door. I hope I'm not calling at a bad time."

He hadn't needed to identify himself because I instantly recognized that deep, melodic voice. "Not at all."

"I have been working from home today, and now that the sun looks like it might be coming out, I was thinking about going out for some lunch. I'm not used to being caged up in the house, and I'm getting cabin fever. Would you like to go with me?"

"I didn't realize it had stopped raining," I said. "I've been working around the house. Lunch sounds good."

"I know it's short notice, but could you be ready to go in about a half hour? If not, we can go later."

"I can be ready. I will see you in a little while."

My heart was doing a little skipping, and I stopped to take a deep breath. I looked at the clothes I had laid out to wear before the call and decided on something a little less casual since I was now going to be with other people, and especially since I was going to be with Simon.

"Oh, come on, Casey," I admonished myself. "It's just lunch, not a marriage proposal. Besides, aren't you the one who has said she wasn't interested in getting married again?" I laughed at my conversation. "It is kind of nice to be asked out, though. I didn't realize what being asked out again after so many years would feel like. It reminds me of my teenage years, although I'm hopefully able to handle things more maturely than I did at sixteen." I took a deep breath and laughed as I finished putting on my makeup and clothes.

"I'm glad you were able to make it, Casey," said Simon as I opened the door. His green eyes lit up, and I was grateful I had chosen the deep purple sweater and gray slacks. "You look really nice."

He opened the door of his blue SUV for me and waited until I was comfortably seated in the soft leather seat.

"If I had known I was taking someone out, I would have gotten the car washed up. It's pretty dusty after going out to job sites," he said as he seated himself a few moments later on the driver's side.

I chuckled. "And then it would have just needed to be washed again after going out on these wet streets."

"You do have a point," he said with a smile. "I have a favorite little place I eat at that specializes in Mexican food, but they do have other non-Mexican dishes, too. How does that sound to you?"

"I haven't had Mexican food in a while. Years ago, it used to practically be a mainstay of my diet. There was a place near where I worked that a group of us would go to when we could get away for lunch. Since I retired, though, I haven't eaten it as much, so I think I enjoy it more than I did."

"How long ago did you retire?"

"Almost eight years. It doesn't seem like it could be that long."

"You must have retired early then," he commented, and then his face reddened. "Sorry, that sounds like a comment on your age."

I laughed. "It doesn't matter to me if it was. I retired at sixty-two after being with the Indian Health Service for thirty-five years. Things were changing in my family, and my husband and I were wanting to do some traveling, so it seemed like a good time to retire. You are still working. Do you enjoy what you do? Not that I think you ought to be retired. You are younger than I am."

"There isn't that much difference in our ages, Casey. I'm sixty-five, so I could retire, but I really do love what I do. I've been in construction since I graduated from high school. I love watching, and being a part of, the whole process. My company builds schools all over the state, and sometimes in other countries."

"Your grandson mentioned to me that you had been building schools somewhere all summer."

"Yes, I was, and Greg was with us for a couple of months. We were building some schools in Mexico for a nonprofit down there."

He pulled into the parking area next to a white-washed adobe building, and after turning the ignition off, he came and opened the door for me.

The place was teeming with business. We were ushered to a small table near a window looking out at a garden where more tables were located but unoccupied because of the weather. The decorations were cheerful in yellows, white, blue, and orange, and made a bright spot on an overcast, chilly day.

Simon was watching me as I took in our surroundings. "What do you think so far?"

"I'm glad you chose this place, Simon. Just looking at it makes me feel good. I didn't quite know what to expect."

"I don't think you will be disappointed in the food either. I've eaten most of what they offer, except the American meals. I figure I can eat those somewhere else. There are a lot of Mexican restaurants in this town, but this is the one I come to if I want Mexican food."

We opened the menus, and my mouth started watering as I read. It had been quite a while since I had eaten Mexican food, as I had told Simon, and it all sounded delicious. I decided on what I wanted fairly quick. When I put down the menu, Simon had already closed his menu, and a waitress came and took our order.

"Did you have some kind of plans for the day that didn't include staying in because of the rain?" Simon asked.

I nodded, and my eyes misted over. I quickly brushed away the moisture. Simon showed alarm, and I held up my hand. "It's all right. I work as a hospice volunteer, and the client I would have been seeing today passed away this morning. I decided to do some work around my house, because of the rain, and might have done it anyway because I didn't have anything else planned."

"That must be hard volunteering for a hospice. I don't know if it is something I could sign up for myself."

"I understand. Working for, or volunteering for, hospice certainly isn't for everyone. My husband was on hospice when he passed away, so I became acquainted with them because of him. Also, my background in nursing probably helped influence my decision. I, on the other hand, have never been able to do construction, and I have a hard time visualizing myself with a tool belt and a hard hat."

Simon laughed. "I can see it, but there is a little bit more to the work than wearing a tool belt and a hard hat."

"What got you started in construction? You said you had been doing it since you graduated from high school."

"I didn't know what I wanted to do when I grew up. My parents were pushing for me to go to college, but I felt like it would be a waste of time and money. It probably would have been. My dad's best friend, Dale, had a construction business, and I went to him and asked if he would hire me. I didn't know anything about construction, but he hired me. I started from the ground up. It was long, excruciating hours, and being a typical high school kid, I wasn't used to that at all. I was tempted to give up many times and go off to school, but I had chosen a different school that made a man out of me. Along the way, I started taking night classes at the junior college, because I wanted to go further with construction and have my own company someday."

"I admire you for taking the time to find out what you really wanted to do instead of doing what you thought others wanted you to do. That takes a lot of courage."

"Or just plain stubbornness," Simon said with a laugh. "I learned a lot along the way, that's for sure. What about you? Did you always want to be a nurse?"

I shook my head. "No. I knew I wanted to go to college, and my father was willing to support me, whatever I decided to do. The options were different for women when I was in high school. I had decided that I would either become a teacher or a nurse. A very wise friend told me that if I became a teacher, I would probably be an old maid, and because I looked good in white, I ought to become a nurse. I certainly didn't want to be an old maid, so I became a nurse."

Simon laughed. "You became a nurse because you looked good in white?"

I joined in his laughter and nodded. "Yes, I did. Do you have any idea how long I wore white?" He shook his head, and I continued. "Maybe for three years. The reason for my choice wasn't the best, but it did end up being the best choice for me. I loved my work until I decided to retire."

When our meal came, it was as good as Simon had promised. We didn't do a lot of talking during the meal. It was an easy, companionable time.

"You aren't from this area, are you?" Simon asked as he put down his fork and took a sip of water.

"No, I moved here from the valley."

"Most people move from here to the valley when they retire, or just live here in the summer. We are kind of a reverse snowbird community. Or maybe, since it hasn't snowed yet, you will be taking off when it does?"

I smiled. "No, I don't have intentions of leaving here when the snow flies. I no longer have a home in the valley. This is my home now."

"I'm glad to hear it."

"How about you? Are you from here, Simon?"

"We moved here when I was fourteen. My dad worked in the oil fields in North Dakota, Montana, and Wyoming, so we had moved around a lot. My mom got tired of being a nomad and the harshness of the winters. They compromised and decided to move here where there are still four seasons, but compared to where we were, the winters are milder." He chuckled. "The compromise went out the window when my dad retired. They both decided they were tired of the winter. They sold everything and bought a motor home. Now they live in a senior living apartment in the valley."

"I guess you never know where you might end up. Someone once told me, 'If you want to make God laugh, make plans.'"

"Would you like some dessert or coffee?"

"No, thanks. I don't think I left room for anything else. It was good food. I will remember this place."

Simon and I walked outside, and I noticed the dark clouds were building up again. "It looks like we may be in for some more rain."

Simon nodded in agreement as he opened the door on his vehicle for me. Before he could get into his side of the car, big drops of rain started falling.

"That was a good break from it. I guess I can go back to my paperwork now that I've had a time of respite from my cabin fever. How about you? Do you have plans for the afternoon?"

142

"It seems like a good day to put on a pot of soup and to start in on the book I have waiting for me. I don't think shopping, or much of anything else, sounds very appealing on a day like today. I guess being retired has its benefits. I don't have to go anywhere unless I want to."

When we arrived back at my home, I tried to convince Simon to stay in the car, but he insisted on getting out his umbrella from the back seat and walking me up to the door.

I laughed when we were up on the porch. "I thought we had agreed that if I went out with you there wouldn't be any waterworks."

His green eyes lit up as he grinned. "I guess I lied. Thanks for going with me, Casey. I'm glad you tempted fate and went out with me."

"Me, too. I had a good time."

He took one of my hands in his larger ones, looked deeply into my eyes, and then squeezed my hand gently before letting it go. "I hope we can do something again. I enjoyed myself. I will try to do something about the water, but it is hard to make promises when mother nature is conspiring against me."

"I would like that, Simon." He started to turn away, and I said, "I know we just ate, but I was wondering if you would like to come over later for some of that soup I'm going to make. I can open an extra can," I said with a laugh.

"Canned soup," he said thoughtfully. "It sounds tempting, and probably a lot better than the brand of soup I have at my house. Maybe I will risk it."

I changed into the clothes I had been going to wear earlier, and I began work on the soup for that evening when the phone rang.

"Hi, Casey, what are you up to? I finished with stuff here at the office and wondered if you would like to get together. I know the weather is a little off-putting, and I'm glad to come over there since I will already be out."

"Hi, Georgia, I would love to see you. Come on over, and you can support me while I make some soup."

Fifteen minutes later, Georgia arrived. She was dressed in jeans and an orange sweater. Her hair was pulled back with a clip.

"It's so good to see you. Did you have something for lunch?"

"Yes, I did. I see you have some coffee. I would love a cup of that." Georgia was almost as familiar with my kitchen as I was. She went to the cupboard and retrieved a mug, filled it with coffee, and then settled on one of the barstools as I continued chopping vegetables. "A pot of soup on a rainy day. That is a perfect idea. I should probably be home making my own. Dave would love it."

"Now, don't go running off, Georgia. You just got here," I said, laughing.

"I won't, because making soup at my house would be more of a project for me. I would have to go grocery shopping first, and then it would probably be midnight before the soup was done."

"I'm grateful I already had the vegetables and everything I needed for the soup before I decided to put this together." I hesitated before continuing. "I had lunch with Simon, and when he brought me home, I invited him to come over for soup this evening."

"Simon?" Georgia asked. "Oh, that's right. Your neighbor you introduced me to the day we had lunch. Tell me more. It's been too long since we've talked. I didn't know you had been seeing Simon."

"Georgia, we talked yesterday," I said, laughing. "Simon and I have not been seeing each other. This lunch was a spontaneous invitation because he was working at home today and wanted a reprieve from being inside. Taking me out to lunch was also a way to take a break."

"That is one way of putting it. I thought you had a visit with your hospice client this morning."

I nodded. "She passed away early this morning, so my plans changed."

"Oh, I'm so sorry, Casey. I know you thought you were starting to make some headway with the husband. Are you doing okay?"

"As a matter of fact, I am. I wasn't totally surprised because when I was there earlier in the week, she slept almost the whole time I was there. Her husband trusted me enough to go out and do some yardwork while I sat with her, so I guess I did make some headway with him. In fact, he was the one who called me to tell me she had died. He was confused about what to do next, so I reminded him to call hospice, and they would support him in taking care of what needed to be done.

"I'm proud of myself, Georgia, because after he called, I took time to feel my feelings and allowed myself a good cry. It's progress for me because when I was dealing with my mother and Richard, all I did was stuff my feelings."

"Yay!" Georgia said as she raised her mug of coffee in salute. "I am proud of you too. Do you think you will continue to volunteer for hospice?"

"Yes, that's my plan. Diana, the volunteer coordinator, called me to let me know my client had passed away, and she told me to take the time I needed to process things. Then when I'm ready to take a new client, I am to give her a call."

While we talked, I continued cutting up vegetables and putting them in a large bowl.

"Can I help do some of the vegetables for you? I will do my best not to bleed on the project."

"Now, that is some offer," I said, laughing. Georgia put down her empty coffee mug, and I gave her a knife. "You can work on the peppers. Just cut them in half, and remove the insides. I'm going to roast all of these vegetables, and I like to roast the peppers in halves so I can take the skins off after they are roasted.

"Georgia, I have to admit to being nervous about seeing someone. I thought about it once in a while when Richard was sick, but then I would feel guilty."

Georgia put her knife down and gave me a hug. "I think it was perfectly natural to think about it, even though Richard was still alive. It was part of your coping mechanism to possibly give yourself some hope for the future."

"I guess it was, although it didn't help in the long run, or I wouldn't have been standing at the Grand Canyon feeling like I wanted to end my life."

"Remember, Casey, you were doing the best you could. You had been through a lot."

"I continue to be grateful to my Three musketeers for rescuing me. Speaking of my Three Musketeers, I love the pictures from Peter and Jacob that they are posting online. It makes me wish I was there with them. Going to New England at this time of year to see the fall colors, and spend time with some of their family was such a great idea."

"I agree. We will have to have a welcome home party when they get back," Georgia said enthusiastically.

"That would be fun. Georgia, this is going to be a big pot of soup. Why don't you and Dave come over and join us?" I asked impulsively.

"Are you sure you want us to come over when you are having a new man over? We might scare him off."

"I will take the chance. Simon and I are just getting to know one another, and if we decide to continue to see each other, I would want him to meet my friends. Then, if he gets scared off, I'll know it wasn't meant to be," I added, laughing.

Georgia texted Dave to make sure he didn't have other plans. When he responded a few minutes later stating he was open to our plans, Georgia and I continued making the soup. The excitement grew as we talked about the coming evening. I told Georgia about how I met Simon, and we had a good laugh.

***

After Georgia left, I decided I would call Simon and let him know I had invited Georgia and Dave to join us for soup. I didn't want to spring them on him unexpectedly, and I wanted to give him an opportunity to change his mind about coming over if having others there with us was not what he wanted. A part of me wondered if I was afraid of being alone with him, and another part of me wondered if I was being disloyal to Richard by desiring to have someone new in my life. I shook my head at my thoughts and called his number.

I left a message on his phone asking him to call me back when his phone went straight to voice mail. He called me back a half an hour later. I had the soup simmering in the slow cooker and the dishes washed.

"Hi, Casey. Did the can opener break?"

"No, the soup is cooking. My friend Georgia came over and helped me put the soup together. I invited her and her boyfriend to come and eat with us. I didn't want to surprise you and have them just show up. Do you mind having another couple here?"

"And miss out on your soup? No way! I've been looking forward to it. I will do my best to be on good behavior."

"That's a relief," I said, chuckling. "I will see you soon."

Chapter 13

Simon arrived and brought me a mixed bouquet of fall flowers. He handed them to me and gave me a kiss on the cheek.

"Something, besides you, smells really good." Simon was wearing a soft brown shirt with the sleeves rolled up to midarm and tan corduroy slacks. His green eyes were sparkling.

"Oh, that must be the cooking oil," I said, more than a little flustered. "Thank you for the flowers. They are so pretty. Let me get something to put them in. Come in and make yourself comfortable. Dave and Georgia will be coming soon. I introduced you to Georgia when I saw you at the restaurant where she and I had been having lunch, and I ... I sound like a babbling teenager."

Simon chuckled. "I like the way you sound. I can understand being nervous when you're getting to know someone, and then you invite that person to meet your friends. Remember, I did promise to be on good behavior tonight."

I smiled and then couldn't help laughing. "I know you did, but after all, you promised not to have waterworks the next time we saw each other too."

My nerves dissipated with the laughter. I went into the kitchen and found a vase to put the flowers in. Simon followed me, and while I put water in the vase, he lifted the lid on the slow cooker. "Wow! This smells a lot better than the cans of soup I buy. You will have to let me know what brand this is." Then he opened the oven door. "I can't believe it, corn bread. I feel like I have died and gone to heaven."

"Simon, you remind me of a little kid at Thanksgiving or Christmas."

"You caught me. I love OPC." He explained when I repeated the initials as I tried to figure out what they meant, "Other people's cooking. OPC. When you have been a bachelor as long as I have, you get tired of your own cooking."

"Would you like a glass of wine or something?"

He shook his head. "No thanks. I'm good. If you have milk, maybe I will have some of that with dinner, or just water is good."

Just then, the doorbell rang, and I went to greet Georgia and Dave, and Simon went with me. I gave each one of them a hug. Simon shook Georgia's hand, and then he turned toward Dave as I introduced Simon to Dave. As Simon shook Dave's hand, he looked at him quizzically. "I think we have met before."

"You nut," Dave said and grabbed Simon for a hug. Georgia and I stood by and watched this exchange.

"I would say introductions seem to have been unnecessary. Come on in, and take off your jackets," I said.

Georgia took Dave's jacket and headed for the bedroom to put them in there. It had stopped raining, but the outside temperature had dropped considerably from what it had been earlier.

Knowing Dave didn't drink alcohol, I had heated some apple cider and had it warming on the stove. I took some shrimp appetizers and crackers out of the fridge and put them on the coffee table. "Would anyone like some apple cider? I have it ready. And I even have cinnamon sticks if you would like one."

We all took a mug of the cider and went into the living room. The fireplace was glowing and lent a feeling of welcome and warmth to the room.

"It feels like a refuge after being out in the cold for a little while," Dave said. "The heater in my car decided to act up on the way over here. I will have to take it in and have it looked at. I will give my mechanic a call in the morning and see if he can take a look at it."

Simon nodded. "With temperatures getting colder, you sure want to make sure the heater is working."

"I agree," Georgia added, "or we'll have to be taking my car."

Dave held up his hand. "I don't think so. After I folded myself into your little car, it would probably take the jaws of life to get me out of there."

A picture of Dave with his chin resting on his knees in Georgia's compact car had all of us laughing.

"I didn't realize you lived over in this direction," Dave said to Simon. "Georgia was telling me we were having dinner with Casey's neighbor, but I had no clue the neighbor would be you."

"We usually talk on the phone or meet up somewhere downtown, so you wouldn't have known," Simon replied. "Usually we try to keep the riffraff out of our neighborhood, but I guess Georgia keeps a tight rein on you," he added with a smile.

"That's kind of the pot calling the kettle black, although I am black, so I can't complain too much." Simon nodded slightly, and Dave continued. "Simon and I are both friends of Bill W. In fact, Simon has been my sponsor now for almost two years. He helped me when I was really in a bad place, and I am eternally grateful.

"It goes both ways, buddy," Simon said. "As I support you, and others, I help myself."

Dave had explained in the past about being a member of Alcoholics Anonymous and that he continued to attend meetings.

"Support is really important when you are going through life's challenges," I agreed.

We finished our cider and appetizers and then wandered into the kitchen. Georgia helped me serve the salad, soup, and cornbread. Lighthearted teasing and conversation continued. I was grateful I had invited Georgia and Dave to join us this evening. After removing the cornbread from the oven, I had slipped in a pan of brownies to bake, and they were the perfect ending to the meal.

"Thank you for this wonderful meal, Casey. I was not expecting a full meal with all the fixings when you invited me earlier. I thought we were just having soup, but I am glad you did. I've eaten enough for two people," Simon added, patting his stomach.

Georgia and Dave had just left after they had insisted on doing the dishes so I wouldn't be left to clean it all up by myself.

"I'm really glad you enjoyed it. I had fun putting it all together."

We went into the living room and sat down on the sofa.

"Casey, I would like to tell you some things about myself. I have enjoyed being with you, and before we spend much more time together, I want you to know about me and what has helped to create who I am today. That way you can choose whether or not you want to continue to see me." His green eyes were serious as he looked at me.

I frowned, and he smoothed my forehead with one of his work-roughened hands. "Don't worry, I'm not a mass murderer or child molester." He sat down about a foot away from me on the sofa.

"I want to let you know why I attend AA and what brought me there. I told you I started working in construction right out of high school," he reminded me, "but I didn't share that little by little I started drinking along with the other guys who were all older than I was. I thought I needed to for them to accept me as one of them.

"I met a girl, and she and I ended up moving in together. She partied right along with me, and then she got pregnant. She quit drinking, but I didn't. The pregnancy woke her up, and she didn't want to harm the baby. We got married because I did want to take responsibility for the baby. It might have been better if we hadn't, but who knows? The baby came, and he really changed my wife's life and the way she saw our lives. Me? All I did was go to work, party, and then come home and pass out. My wife couldn't take it. She tried to get me to go to AA, but I refused to see that I had a drinking problem.

"When Chad was nine months old, she left me and took him with her. It took me five more years before I woke up, and by then Tina had married someone else. Once I started attending AA, I met with her, and we arranged for me to have visiting rights with Chad. As you can imagine, since I hadn't had much to do with him up until that time, it took Chad a while to warm up to having me in his life.

"That's also when I took a good look at my life and decided I didn't like what I saw. I enrolled in the night school classes and then attended college to get my engineering degree."

I took Simon's hand in mine. "I don't know why you would think I would be scared off by your story. What I'm hearing is a hero's journey of persistence and courage. I'm not saying you did things perfectly," I inserted when he started to interrupt me, "but I admire how you took a good look at where you were and the path you were on and decided to do what it took to change things around. Thank you for being willing to share your story with me. I'm not scared and don't see a reason to be." I squeezed his hand gently.

His voice was gruff with emotion when he responded. He turned his hand over and held my hand in his. "It's been a long time since I have allowed myself to share my story with a woman, other than the AA meetings. Our meetings are mostly men, and it is not a good practice to get involved with women who are a part of the group. It adds a dimension to recovery for both that is not always healthy."

We sat in silence for a while gazing at the glow of the fireplace, and then Simon interjected a question about what had brought me to where I am now. I thought about how to answer him and then shared with him about my work as a nurse, about caring for my mother and then my husband, and finally, about being saved from committing suicide and how Jacob, Peter, and Georgia had become my lifeline that supported me in recovery.

Simon listened to me attentively and unconsciously stroked my hand as I revealed to him some of the pain I had endured. Some of the story I had not even shared with my Three Musketeers in the past, and I brushed away moisture away from my eyes. "Sorry, I didn't mean to get all weepy on you."

Simon put a finger to my mouth to silence the apology. "There is nothing to apologize for. You went through a very painful time." He gently pulled me into an embrace, kissed me on the top of my head, and held me for a couple of minutes. It felt so good to be held and nurtured.

As he released me, I smiled crookedly and said, "I had no idea we were going to have such a serious conversation, but I'm glad we did. Thanks for holding me too. It really helped give me comfort and release from the story. I'm really glad you trusted me with your story and that we had this time together."

"I feel the same way, Casey. I've enjoyed myself a lot, and I am glad you invited Dave and Georgia too. It was fun to see Dave and to meet the woman he is in love with. He had mentioned her name, but I didn't connect it when you introduced me to Georgia at that restaurant." He stood up and gently pulled me to my feet. "It is time for me to go." With those words, he put his arms around me and kissed me, and I returned the embrace and the kiss.

***

I didn't feel fully awake after having a late night. My mind was groggy as I sipped on my coffee and attempted to wake up. I had decided to make some waffles. The waffle iron was heating up as I stirred the batter. I was sorely tempted to return to the warmth of my bed and make the waffles later. I shrugged and poured some of the batter into the iron, and a knock sounded at the door.

I opened the door to a smiling Simon. I was embarrassed about still being in my flannel pajamas and slippers, my hair practically standing on end.

"I obviously wasn't expecting company," I said stiffly, as I motioned to my hair and clothes.

"No problem. I guess I should have called before coming over, but I wanted to ask you about something and didn't stop to call. I will remember next time." He sniffed the air. "Do I smell something burning?"

"Oh no!" I turned from him, raced back into the kitchen, and quickly flipped open the waffle maker. I took the waffle out with a fork and threw it in the sink.

"I'm really sorry. I didn't mean to ruin your breakfast."

"It doesn't matter. I have plenty of batter. I can make more. Now, I believe you said something about something you wanted to ask me?"

He looked at me for a moment, as if trying to decide if it was such a good idea, and I said, "Would you like a cup of coffee? If you are hungry, I will make you a waffle."

"I didn't come over to mooch breakfast off of you, but since you are offering, I accept."

I poured him a cup of coffee and said, "I will be back in a couple of minutes to make the waffles. I will feel less self-conscious if I at least comb my hair and put on some clothes."

After changing into jeans and a sweater and attempting to tame my wild hair, I returned to the kitchen. Simon was sitting on one of the stools at the counter with his coffee in front of him. "You didn't have to change on my account, but I'm glad you did if it makes you feel more comfortable."

I poured fresh batter into the waiting waffle maker and poured us both more coffee.

"Would you like to go to Sedona with me today? It doesn't take very long to get there from here, and with the weather on the cold side, there will probably be fewer tourists hanging around. I know it is short notice, but I think it would be fun."

"I love Sedona, and ordinarily, I stay away from there on weekends or holidays, but since it's chilly weather, you are probably right about the tourists. What time are you thinking about going?" I removed the lightly browned waffle and handed the plate to Simon. "Here's some butter and syrup."

He looked at his watch and frowned slightly as he thought. "It's almost eight. If we left here about ten, would that give you enough time to do whatever you need to do?"

I nodded. "I didn't have much planned for today, particularly since I did my housework yesterday that I was going to do today." I poured batter for another waffle, put the pitcher into the sink, and rinsed it off. "What do you have planned?"

"There is one particular place I like to go when I visit there that I thought you might enjoy. It is outside, though. It's a stupa and peace park. We wouldn't have to stay long if the weather makes it too uncomfortable. If there is anything you want to see or do, I'm open to it."

"I've heard of the stupa, but I've never been there. I think I would like it." I fetched the waffle and carried my plate over to join Simon at the counter. "Do you want more coffee?"

"Not for me, but thanks." He carried his now-empty plate to the sink. "Thanks for feeding me." He swiveled my chair around and planted a kiss on my mouth. "I will see you in a couple of hours."

An hour later I finished dressing, and I went to answer my phone. I looked at the caller ID and was surprised to see Simon's number. "I'm not quite ready yet," I said without preamble.

"Casey, I apologize. Something has come up with work, and I have to go to Colorado." His voice sounded defensive, as if he thought she was going to be upset with him for changing our plans.

"I understand. I'm disappointed. I feel sad we aren't going to be able to spend the time together, and I also know we can go to Sedona another time."

Simon didn't speak for a moment, and I was almost afraid he had hung up. His voice had changed to wonder. "You're something, Casey. I was sure you would be upset with me for not being able to go today, especially since I barged in on you this morning. Most people would be upset."

I laughed. "I guess I'm not most people. I really wanted to go, and I know you did too. I've learned that sometimes life can throw a curveball into our plans, and it's up to us in how we decide to handle it."

We ended the call a few minutes later, and I finished getting ready for the day. I decided to go shopping and to stop at the library for something new to read.

Half an hour later I opened the front door just as Simon was about to knock on my door. I wasn't expecting there to be anyone there, and I jumped back and dropped my purse.

"Sorry, Casey," Simon said as he reached down and retrieved the purse for me at the same time I bent down, and we bumped heads. "I'm sorry. Did I hurt you?" he asked as I rubbed the top of my head. "This isn't going the way I hoped."

"Simon," I said, chuckling, "you didn't hurt me. I just wasn't expecting there to be someone at the door when I opened it."

He touched the spot on my head gently and put his arms around me. He kissed the top of my head and then kissed me on my mouth. "This is why I came by. I didn't want to leave town without seeing you. Would it be all right with you if I called you from Denver? I don't know exactly how long this is going to take. Hopefully not more than a couple of days."

"I will look forward to your call," I said, and I put a hand on each one of his cheeks and looked into his eyes. "Travel safe." Then I kissed him.

"Oh, I wish I didn't have to go, but I do. I will call you this evening, Casey." He gave me a quick hug and then walked to his truck. It was parked in my driveway with the engine running. He waved at me before backing the truck into the street, and I stayed where I was like a mariner's wife watching her husband sail away.

***

I went to the library first and found a couple of books to read. Then I decided to stop for a cup of coffee at a coffee shop before doing the shopping I had decided to do. I took one of the books in with me and opened it up after I sat down with my coffee. I opened the book but didn't start reading. A thought occurred to me: *Maybe the universe is telling us to slow down a little.* I took a sip of coffee and thought, *Darn! It's probably a good thing, but I'm like a little kid. I don't want to. I want what I want when I want it.* I laughed to myself and picked up the book again.

I had trouble returning my thoughts to the book. After reading the same paragraph several times, I decided I would give Georgia a call to see if she would like to join me.

"Hey, Georgia," I said as my friend answered the phone. "I'm at Riley's having a cup of coffee and wondered what you are doing. Any chance you would like to go shopping with me?"

"That sounds like fun. Dave is on call today, and he just left to go see a client. I can be there in about ten minutes."

"I have a library book, so take your time. Do you want me to order you a cup of coffee while I'm waiting?"

"That sounds heavenly. I will be there soon."

By the time Georgia arrived, her coffee was waiting for her, and I had received a refill on my own. I stood up and gave her a hug. "I'm so glad you could meet me. Shopping with someone else is so much more fun, and the two of us always have a good time. Besides, you help me stay on track instead of buying the store out."

"It goes both ways, my friend. I admit I was surprised to receive your call. I thought you might be sleeping in today."

"No such luck," I said, shaking my head, "although I did sleep about half an hour later than usual. I was still trying to wake up when I was fixing my breakfast and received an early-morning visitor."

"An early-morning visitor," Georgia said as she took a sip of her coffee. "Tell me more."

I proceeded to tell her about Simon's visit and was grateful I had her to share my tumultuous feelings with. Georgia listened attentively as I talked about the plans Simon and I had made to go to Sedona, and then his needing to leave for Colorado on unexpected business. I ended by talking to her about the idea that had come to me as I sat here in the coffee shop a little while before I called her.

"It occurred to me his needing to leave on business might be the universe's way of telling us to slow things down, although my hormones are protesting." I laughed. "I didn't know I still had hormones to protest."

"I can see why you might be surprised," Georgia said with a smile. "They have probably just been banked in the background waiting for you to come alive again. As for the message from the universe, I guess it's a possibility. I do know that God, or the universe, whatever you want to call it, desires the highest and best for both of you. As someone once said, 'It's hard to see the whole picture when you are in the frame.' I'm excited for you, Casey, no matter what the two of you decide about your relationship in the future."

"Thank you. I knew I could count on you. Are you ready for shopping?"

***

I was engrossed in the library book I had checked out earlier in the day, with my tea growing cold on the table beside me, when my phone rang. "Hello," I said distractedly.

"Hey, Casey, did I wake you up?"

"Oh no, Simon. I was reading, and it took me a moment to pull myself out of the story. It's good to hear your voice. How did your trip go?"

"No problems. The plane was ready when I arrived at the airport and was only waiting for me to be able to take off."

"They held a plane for you to get there?"

"No, silly girl," he said, chuckling. "The plane is mine. My pilot had submitted the flight plan and had everything ready to go.

Sometimes I need to make last-minute trips, so it is handy to have my own plane, rather than depending upon commercial flights."

"You don't pilot it yourself?"

"No, I don't have a pilot's license and have no desire to get one. I'm lucky to have Paul because he is flexible about his hours. He is retired from the air force, is single, and loves to fly. We had some turbulence over the mountains, and it was snowing in Denver when we landed. Otherwise, the trip was pretty smooth."

"I'm glad to hear it. I had wondered if you were driving. We didn't talk about how you were going to travel."

"Sometimes I do drive, but I wanted to meet with our client as soon as I could and get things taken care of. I'm glad I didn't with this storm that came through. I wouldn't have wanted to be caught in it."

"Were you able to meet with the client?"

"No, I decided to go out to the jobsite and talk to my project manager first. I could see firsthand what we were talking about and get Zeke's take on it, and then I called the client and made an appointment to see him. We are going to meet tomorrow morning at the site, along with Zeke, and start figuring things out from there. That's about all there is to tell you now. Tomorrow I will be able to share our progress.

"By the way, thanks for asking. It is strange and fun for me to have someone to share things like this with."

"You are welcome. I like hearing about it and being your listening post."

"What about you? What did you end up doing with your day?"

I shared with Simon about finding a couple of books at the library and inviting Georgia to go shopping with me. He groaned and said, "I'm glad you have a friend to go shopping with. I can't imagine spending hours going in and out of little shops."

Laughing, I agreed. "I would have a hard time seeing you doing it, but you never can tell. You might just have fun too."

It was fun sharing with Simon, and when we finally said good night, I glanced at the time in surprise, realizing we had been talking for over an hour. My book was still open. I no longer felt the desire to read, so I put a bookmark in place and closed it. I took my cup back to the kitchen and reheated my tea in the microwave before heading back into the living room to curl up on the sofa with an afghan wrapped around me.

I felt relaxed and contented. It had been a long time since I had someone, and not just a someone but a man, I could share my day with. It felt good. I smiled as I remembered our conversation and laughter.

Chapter 14

"Oh, Jacob, it seems like you guys have been gone forever. I've missed seeing you. Speaking on the phone just isn't the same as being able to be with you in person."

Jacob laughed. "Wow, Casey! You would have thought we had been gone for months, instead of weeks, and," he added with a pause, "I feel the same way, and I know Peter does too. In fact, that's why I'm calling. We've decided to have a Halloween party on Friday, and it wouldn't be the same without you. Peter is talking to Georgia and Dave about it now."

"That sounds like fun, I think," I said hesitantly. "Do we have to come in costume?"

"No, but you can if you want. A better idea is some kind of silly mask. You can do what you want. The whole idea is for all of us to get together and catch up."

"Count me in. At least I have a couple of days to decide what the appropriate attire would be for your party. I'm looking forward to it. I want to hear the details of your trip, and I hope you have more pictures to share too."

"If the weather holds up, we are going to have a fire in the firepit and have gooey marshmallows and chocolate."

I laughed. "That sounds perfect. Why don't I bring the ingredients for those?" We talked about the party and how good it would be for the Three Musketeers, and company, to be back together again. As the call ended, my phone rang again.

"Hello, Simon, how has your day been?"

"Long," he answered, and I could hear the weariness in his voice. "You sound chipper. How are things with you?"

"I'm a popular woman this evening," I said, laughing. "Two phone calls, one right after the other, from special people. Jacob called to tell me they are home from their trip, and they are putting together a party to celebrate."

"Jacob is one of your friends you told me about who helped you, right?"

"Yes, he and his husband, Peter, were there at the Grand Canyon for me. I'm here today because of them. I hope you will be back from your trip by Friday so you will be able to go to their party with me. Georgia and Dave will be there too. You sound tired. Have you had a rough day?"

"I have. You know, Casey, I'm tired and out of sorts. I don't really feel like talking tonight. I will call you tomorrow."

"Oh. Okay. I will talk to you then.

I looked at the phone after we had disconnected the call. "That's strange. Last night it seemed to help him when we talked about things. Oh well. I hope he gets some rest."

***

The next morning, I decided to call Hospice of the Pines to see if they had someone else I could help with my volunteering.

"Hi, Diana, this is Casey Granger. I wanted to let you know I'm ready for a new client when you have one for me."

"I'm glad to hear it. I have a request that came into the office about an hour ago. It is for an elderly man who came onto hospice a couple of days ago. His wife and daughter are caring for him at home. He has dementia."

"I will come over and pick up the paperwork. I have a few errands to run."

"Great. Do you have a little time for a cup of coffee? It's been a while since we have talked, and I would enjoy touching base with you."

"I would enjoy that. I can be there in about thirty minutes. Would that work for you?"

"Perfect, Casey, I will see you then."

***

When I arrived at Hospice of the Pines, I waved at Steve, who was on a telephone call, and headed in the direction of Diana's office. I stopped at the kitchen and poured myself a cup of coffee along the way.

"Oh, Casey, it is so good to see you. How are you doing? Anything new going on with you?"

"It's good to see you, too, Diana. I'm doing well. I started seeing someone, which is something I wasn't sure I would ever do. It has brought a breath of fresh air. I don't know if anything will happen with it, but that is okay too."

"How fun. I'm glad for you."

"I'm eager to start working with another family, and I'm glad you have another family in mind for me."

Diana handed me the paperwork and said, "As I said on the phone, his wife and daughter have been caring for him by themselves. They are both ready for a break. The daughter is concerned about her mother because her mom's health has started to deteriorate. The daughter is hoping that having a volunteer come in will give her a chance to take her mother out of the house. The mother has been reluctant to leave his bedside, so we will see how it works out."

I nodded. "I can certainly understand how both the wife and daughter feel because of my own experience. Maybe having someone to listen to her will help the wife feel more secure about being away from her husband for a little while. I look forward to hearing what they think will be the most valuable contribution I can make to serve them."

"I will let their team know you are on board then, Casey."

Before I left, Diana gave me the date of the next volunteer gathering. It would be a chance for me to see some of the other volunteers I had been in training with, and I was looking forward to it.

***

After going to the bank and the grocery store, I returned home and placed a call to the home of the Fitzgeralds.

"Hello, this is Casey. I'm a volunteer with Hospice of the Pines."

"Thank you for calling. My name is Morgan Childs. I'm Henry and Mabel's daughter. I'm glad they were able to find a volunteer so quickly. The social worker wasn't sure how long it would take. I guess they don't like to make promises that it will happen right away."

"You're right, Morgan. They wouldn't want to tell you something and then not be able to do it. I'm calling to see when a good time would be for me to come and see you and your parents."

"Would tomorrow morning be all right? Mornings are Dad's best time, and Mom will be more rested too. How about ten?"

"It works for me. I look forward to meeting all of you, Morgan."

***

I was watching an old movie and laughing at some of the antics going on when Simon called that evening. I turned it off as I answered the phone. "Hi, Simon. It's good to hear your voice."

"It's good to hear yours too. It has been a long day, and hearing your voice is like sunshine on a cloudy day."

Simon talked to me about the challenges they were having with his client and some structural changes the client was insisting upon. These changes had not been a part of the original agreement and would require them to go back to ground zero on that part of the building. I was glad to be there for him to have someone to talk to about it.

"Thanks, Casey, for allowing me to bend your ear about all of this. Maybe now I can let go of it and get some sleep," he said with a yawn.

I chuckled. "It sounds like you are ready."

"Yes, I believe you are right. Sorry, I didn't even ask you about your day. What a bore I have turned out to be!"

"Don't worry about it. I will catch you up when we talk again."

"I will talk to you tomorrow. Have a good rest of your evening, Casey."

***

I parked my car in an open spot and walked toward the double-wide mobile home of the Fitzgeralds. The GPS found the location of the mobile home park, but once I was in the park, it was challenging to find their particular place. The front door opened before I even knocked.

"Hello, you are Casey, right? I'm Morgan. Please come in." Morgan was somewhere probably in her late forties, early fifties, with brown hair sprinkled with gray. Her hair was pulled back into a roll at the back of her head. She was wearing a blue and gray dress and athletic shoes.

"Thank you, Morgan."

"This is my mother, Mabel Fitzgerald," she said, putting her arm around a woman that had the appearance of fine china and easily breakable. Mabel was thin, with thinning gray hair and raised blue veins standing out on her birdlike arms and hands. Her faded blue eyes questioned what I was doing there.

"Mrs. Fitzgerald, I'm glad to meet you," I said as I gently took her hand in mine. "I'm a volunteer. They have asked me to come and see if there is any way I could help you and your family."

"Mom, I told you she was coming," Morgan said, and I could hear the frustration in her voice.

"I forgot," Mabel said, with her eyes cast down. "You can call me Mabel. No one calls me Mrs. Fitzgerald. Henry is over here," she said, and she walked to the hospital bed positioned in the living room."

"We had them put the hospital bed in here so Dad could be a part of what is going on, instead of having to be back in the bedroom somewhere," explained Morgan. "He kept having falls, and so we also thought it would be a good idea to be able to see him easily." She went to the man lying with his head elevated and covers pulled up to his armpits, with his arms lying outside of the blankets. "Dad, there's a lady here to see you."

He looked up at her but didn't speak. Then his eyes went to his hands that started fidgeting and picking at the covers.

Morgan turned toward me. "He doesn't talk anymore," she said, "and he isn't eating hardly anything."

"Hello, Mr. Fitzgerald, my name is Casey Granger," I said, approaching the bed slowly. He looked at me apprehensively. "I've come to see if I can help you and your family." I knew from my own experience with my husband, and from the hospice training, that any change in the environment could cause fear to erupt in the person with dementia, so I approached him slowly and did not attempt to touch him. Seeing him fidget with his fingers, and then some restlessness with his legs, let me know he was probably fearful. "I know it can be scary when someone new comes. I understand." Slowly he became quieter.

"See, Mom," Morgan said. "She knows how to be with Dad. You and I could go out and have a cup of coffee or something. Dad will be safe with Casey. We can call home and see how he is doing if we want to, and we can give Casey my cell number so she can call us if she needs to get a hold of us."

"Not today, Morgan," Mabel said, shaking her head. "I'm so tired. I don't really want to go anywhere."

"Why don't you go take a nap then? I do have a couple of errands I want to do. Casey can stay here with Dad," she said, glancing over at me, and I nodded.

Mabel hesitated for a moment. "You will come and get me if he needs me?" she asked me.

"Yes, I will."

"Okay, then. I will go lie down, although I probably won't go to sleep."

I saw a blanket and pillow at one end of the sofa, and Morgan said in explanation, "That's where she sleeps, and I know she isn't getting very much sleep. I hear her up and around at all hours. They have been married for sixty years and have been pretty much inseparable since he retired twenty years ago."

"I have your number, Morgan, and I will call you if anything comes up."

"Thank you, Casey. He's had his meds, although he doesn't get much, and a few bites of breakfast, so he shouldn't need anything. Is there anything you need?"

"No, I've brought a book to read. I'm fine."

"Thank you so much," Morgan said, and she gave me a hug. "You have no idea how much this means so me," she added, wiping at her eyes. "I've been worried every time I leave here. I'm as concerned for her as I am for my father."

"I'm glad to be here to support you, as well as your parents."

Morgan changed her shoes and put on a coat. "Oh! Brrr! It seems like it's getting colder out here. I will see you in a little while."

I stood in the door for a brief moment. She was right. It was sleeting, and I wondered if it was only going to get colder.

After a few minutes, Henry stopped fidgeting, turned on his side away from me, and curled up in a fetal position. I gently repositioned his blanket to make sure he was covered and noticed that his eyes were closed.

Hazel came into the living room about an hour later and went straight to the bed. Henry was still sleeping. She looked up at me sleepily and then back down at her husband. "I'm glad he's sleeping," she whispered. "What did you say your name was?"

"My name is Casey. Were you able to sleep?"

She nodded. "I didn't think I was going to, but I did. Would you like a cup of tea?"

"Thank you. May I help you with it?" I followed her toward the kitchen area, and she asked, "Would you get the teapot off that shelf? Usually I would just heat up some water for one cup, but this would be nicer."

I watched as she put a tea kettle onto the stove, retrieved a couple of flowered teacups, and put out some cookies on a plate. "My daughter helped me make these yesterday." When the water was hot, I lifted the kettle off the stove and poured the water into the teapot for her. Mabel then put a couple of tea bags into the pot and secured the strings with the lid so they wouldn't drop into the water.

"This is fun," Mabel said. "Morgan doesn't care for tea, so usually it's just me now since Henry doesn't drink tea or much of anything else." Her eyes filled with tears, and I put my arms around her thin shoulders.

"I'm sorry you are going through this, Mabel. You two have been married for so many years, and I can only imagine what this is like for you."

Mabel sniffed and got a handkerchief out of her pocket, wiped her eyes, and blew her nose. "It's hard. I've known Henry since we were in grade school. We attended a one-room schoolhouse out in the country and then rode a bus into town to high school. That was a long time ago."

When the tea was steeped, I carried the pot into the living room and placed it on the coffee table, where Mabel had indicated. She brought the teacups and then went back for the cookies and sugar bowl.

Mabel stood by the bed and looked down at her husband, smoothed his hair, and then came to sit next to me on the sofa. "I like sitting here where I can watch him. I imagine Morgan probably told you that I have been sleeping on the couch, so I can hear Henry if he needs anything. He has always been so good to me. It's the least I can do for him."

We had just finished our tea and taken the teapot back to the kitchen when Morgan returned. Her cheeks were rosy from the cold, and her nose was dripping. "I should have worn warmer clothes," she said as she kicked off her shoes. "It's a mess out there."

Morgan was absolutely correct, and I too regretted not wearing my heavier coat when I had come out earlier. As I pulled into my driveway and opened the garage door electronically, the heater in my car finally started working. It had been snowing heavily, and I had had to chip the ice off the windshield before leaving the Fitzgeralds. I was shivering with cold and grateful to finally be home.

I soon had coffee making and the fireplace sending out warmth. I was thankful I didn't have to wait for a wood fire to get going.

A knock sounded at the door. I looked out and was surprised to see Simon standing on the porch.

"Come in, Simon. It's so good to see you," I said, giving him a hug.

"I tried to call you but you didn't answer, so I could let you know I was back. I saw you come home, and I thought I would come over rather than call again."

"I had my phone with me, and it didn't ring," I said, perplexed. I pulled it out of my pocket. "Oh, no! I forgot to take it off silent. I was with my new hospice client. I muted it because both he and his wife were sleeping, and I didn't want it to disturb them. I'm sorry I missed your call, but I'm really glad to be seeing you in person."

"Your hospice client," Simon repeated. "I would have thought you weren't going to do that anymore since it upset you when your last one died. It's pretty hard on you. I didn't like seeing you upset. Maybe you should have them get someone else for the case, and you should stop putting your heart out there to get broken."

I couldn't believe what I was hearing. I shook my head. "You don't know me, or understand me, Simon. I love doing this work. I love being able to support people who are going through these types of challenges, and I'm darn good at it."

"You are right. I don't really know you, and for sure, I don't understand you. This guy will croak too, and that leaves you right back at square one."

"I guess it does, but it is my choice. I'm glad you came to let me know you're back. I'm tired, though, and I think I would like to be by myself."

"Okay, Casey. Sorry, I didn't mean things to turn out this way. Maybe we can talk tomorrow."

I was relieved when he left. I sat down in a chair and put my head between my hands. *I put up with men in my life trying to tell me what to do and how I should feel in the past. I'm not going to let it happen again.*

Chapter 15

The next morning, I called and left a message for Simon. It had stopped snowing. I didn't know if he would be working from home or not, but I did want to have a conversation with him as soon as possible.

I dressed in warm clothes, a heavy jacket, boots, and gloves and went out to tackle the snow on my porch steps, sidewalk, and driveway. Shoveling snow was something I had never done before, but I was prepared. I put my phone in my pocket in case Simon called back, and I made sure it was not silenced.

There was a cold breeze blowing, and I thought I might turn into a snowman as I put my shovel to work clearing the snow. I was beginning to regret not purchasing a snowblower the man at the hardware store had suggested. At the time I had imagined myself out in the snow effortlessly, and kind of romantically, removing the snow. Since I hadn't lived in a place where you experience snow, or the four seasons, I hadn't thought about how cold and miserable it might actually be while doing the actual snow removal. I had to admit I was certainly getting a good workout without being at the gym.

An hour later, I was done and knocking the snow off my boots against the step when my phone rang.

"Hi, Casey, I just got your message. What's up?"

"Are you working at home today? I want to get together and talk."

"I will be home in about an hour. I have a few minutes now if you would like to talk about whatever it is."

"Thanks, but I would prefer to speak to you in person."

"You sound pretty serious," he commented. "You have my curiosity stoked. I will be there in an hour, and we can talk."

After taking a warm shower and getting dressed, I put on a pot of coffee. I sat down on the sofa in my favorite spot to gather my thoughts about what I wanted to say to Simon. I watched the flame in the fireplace and meditated. This was a conversation where I definitely wanted to be pre-prayered, clear, and centered.

True to his word, it was exactly an hour after our conversation when Simon knocked on my door. I returned his hug and said, "Come in, Simon. I have fresh coffee if you would like a cup." I poured a cup for each of us and then pulled a chair out from the dining room table. I set his cup on the table in front of a chair to the right of mine.

He took off his heavy jacket and hung it on the back of a chair before taking the offered seat.

"Thanks for coming. I really appreciate it."

"You're welcome. What did you want to talk about?" he asked after taking a sip of coffee.

"Simon, it has been really fun for me to spend time with you, and I have enjoyed our conversations," I started.

"I sense a 'but' coming." Simon put down his coffee cup. His green eyes questioned what this was all about without.

"It's not a 'but,' because that would negate my words. I have enjoyed our times together, and I want to have a conversation about the conversation we had yesterday." I held up a hand to stop him from interrupting as I continued. "Yesterday you verbalized your opinion about me volunteering for hospice and that I should resign and let someone else take the new family I am seeing."

He nodded. "I think it is too hard on you. You like to read—why not volunteer at the library or somewhere where you won't get hurt."

"I appreciate your concern, and you have a right to your opinion, but you don't know me well enough to know what the right thing for me is. I'm made of much stronger stuff than you are aware of.

"For a good part of my life, I have had male figures in my life dictating to me what is best for me. A little over a year ago, that ended. I now make decisions for myself about myself. I am fully capable of discerning what is best for me or not." I smiled briefly as I continued. "I'm not a fragile flower that needs to be protected in a hothouse.

"Yes, I love to read, and I appreciate librarians and those who volunteer at the library, but that wouldn't make my heart sing. Working as a hospice volunteer does. I love being with these people who are going through life's challenges and being a support for them.

"Working as a nurse for more than thirty-five years and taking care of my mother and husband through their dementia journeys prepared me for this volunteering."

Simon shook his head. "I don't think I've met anyone like you before," he admitted. "You brought out all of my desires to protect and shelter. I don't want you to get hurt, and that's why I responded the way I did."

"I hear that, Simon, and I don't need to be protected and sheltered."

"So where do we go from here? Are you saying you don't want to go out with me anymore?"

"I can see why you might think that," I said with a smile. I stood up and brought the coffeepot over to refresh his coffee and add more to my own cup. After sitting back down, I continued. "What I would like to do is be friends and get to know each other. Then we will be able to decide whether we would like the relationship to be more than that." I chuckled. "I have to admit my own hormones, which I didn't know were still active, came alive, and I thought I was ready to go full speed ahead."

"You weren't alone in that," Simon agreed with a laugh.

"I am grateful your trip helped to slow things down. I would rather have you for a good friend than a onetime lover. Do you get what I'm saying?"

"I think so," he answered slowly. "You've given me a lot to consider and mull over, Casey. It wasn't what I wanted to hear, but I think I understand."

He stood up and started to put on his jacket, then stopped. I stood up. He put his jacket on the chair, came over, put his arms around me, and kissed the top of my head. "Thanks for the coffee, Casey, and for having this conversation. I don't know where it will go from here, but I do want to respect what you have said and give it some thought."

"Thank you. I appreciate it."

After Simon left, I had mixed feelings about our conversation. I knew in my heart the conversation was the best thing, and I was uncomfortable not knowing what would happen next. A part of me wanted to call him back, but most of all, I knew this was the best thing for both of us right now. I didn't want to have a relationship with anyone that was not healthy for either of us.

I called Georgia. "Any chance you would be able to meet me for lunch? I still haven't found the perfect mask for Jacob and Peter's party. Maybe we could hunt for one of those, although I could probably find one at the grocery store. They had plenty of Halloween stuff the last time I was there."

"It sounds like a plan. With the sun up and warm, the snow is starting to melt, so it is going to be a pretty day. At least, that is what I have decided."

Forty-five minutes later Georgia and I met at one of our favorite spots. Other people seemed to be wanting to get out, so the café was busy. We were able to get one of the last booths. We placed our orders, and then Georgia asked, "What's going on besides wanting to get a mask for the party this evening?"

"You know me pretty well, my friend," I answered with a smile. "How do you know I wasn't just craving some girl time?"

"Because I do know you."

I took a deep breath. "I had a conversation with Simon this morning. I initiated it," I said as I swiped at my moist eyes. "I told him we needed to chill our jets for a while." Georgia nodded, and I continued. "When I told him I would be seeing another family on hospice, he said I should quit volunteering for hospice and have someone else see this family. He said he didn't want me to get hurt again, and that maybe I could volunteer at the library or something.

"Georgia, you know how much volunteering for hospice has meant to me, and volunteering at a library, or something, would not be fulfilling for me at all.

"I told him that I appreciated his concern and that I know better than anyone else what is the best thing for me. A few years ago, I would have listened to him and did what he wanted me to do. It sounds codependent, doesn't it? And I am not that person anymore."

"I hear how courageous you were in setting boundaries for yourself, Casey. I know you were really enjoying being with him."

"I was," I said, nodding. "I never imagined getting into a relationship with someone at my age. Now I know the old saying, 'There may be snow on the roof, but there's fire in the furnace,' is true. I felt happy and alive in a different way than I have been for a long time. Now I also know there are possibilities for me still."

Georgia laughed. "There certainly are. How did you leave it with Simon?"

"It was a surprise for him, and he said he needs to think things over. He did ask if I would still be interested in going out with him, and I told him I was. I let him know we just need to slow things down. We will see what happens."

"I'm really proud of you, Casey, for standing up for yourself and letting Simon know what is important to you." She toasted me with her glass of water, and we clinked glasses and laughed.

"Now, about this mask for the party."

Chapter 16

Dave's car was already parked in Jacob and Peter's driveway when I arrived, and there were a couple of other cars I didn't recognize parked in the street. Jacob saw me through the window and came out to give me a bear hug, soon followed by Peter.

"Hello, my pretties," I said with a high-pitched voice. "It's so good to see you both! Would you like a bite of my apple?" My mask was a rendition of a wicked queen with a large wart on the end of the nose. I was carrying an apple.

"I should have brought a taxi so you wouldn't have recognized me."

"It's true," Peter said as he gave me a hug. "That mask distracts so much from the rest of you, we wouldn't have noticed the person wearing it."

"You two are sure dressed for the occasion."

Peter was dressed as a chef with a tall, oversized, cylindrical chef's hat and a long white apron that reached almost to his ankles. He wore a white mask covering his eyes and had rubbed flour on his cheeks.

Jacob had on jeans, a leather vest, a sheriff's star, a large Stetson, and a plastic toy water gun in a holster. "It's up to me to round up everybody and bring them into the gathering."

"He wanted to wear spurs, but I nixed that. I didn't want us to end up with people getting hurt or scratching up the furniture," said Peter. "Come on in, and we will introduce you to some of our other friends."

It was a fun party. I enjoyed meeting Peter and Jacob's friends, as well as seeing Georgia and Dave. I wished things were different with Simon and me because it would have been fun to share this time with him. I hadn't seen him since our conversation of the day before. I shrugged inside and joined in on the laughter and games. My mask won first place in the category of being the most unlike my own character. Everyone won first place in some kind of category that Peter and Jacob had made up, so we all sported blue ribbons. I couldn't remember the last time I had laughed so much.

***

On Sunday, I decided to go to the church where Georgia was the associate minister. Something inside of me had been telling me this would be a good thing for me. Georgia had not tried to influence me about coming to her church. She knew it was up to me to decide if this was what I wanted to do. I was intrigued by the things she had told me off and on, but I had never felt compelled to go. I knew it was time for me to expand my relationships to other people, and spending time in a spiritual atmosphere would support me finding people with similar beliefs.

I had dressed in gray, soft wool slacks and an aqua-colored cashmere sweater with a cowl collar. I found a place to sit and took my coat off. There was a musical group playing lively music, and it felt welcoming to me. A couple of different women introduced themselves to me with warm smiles of greeting.

Georgia did a double take as she started to walk by where I was sitting. "I didn't expect to see you. I'm so glad you came," she said, laughing as she gave me a warm hug. "I have some things I am doing early in the service, and then I will come back and sit with you." She left her purse and a water bottle and then took a seat in front next to another woman, whom I rightly presumed was the senior minister, even though I had never met her before.

During the announcements, I heard about a silent retreat being held at a retreat center in Prescott. *I wonder if I could be silent for three days*, I thought to myself. I had heard about them in the past but had never gone to one. The senior minister, Peggy Sloan, would be leading the retreat, and after hearing her positive message about selfcare where she had us laughing at her own personal stories, and inviting us to take a look at our own lives, I decided I wanted to attend the retreat. I wondered if Georgia was planning to attend.

When the service ended, Georgia and I joined the line of people waiting to greet Rev. Sloan, and Georgia introduced her to me. "Peggy, this is my good friend Casey. This is her first time here."

"I'm glad you came, Casey. I saw you sitting with Georgia. It is nice to meet you." Her deep blue eyes were warm with welcome. She was slender and about four inches taller than I. Her shoulder-length brown hair was highlighted with blond and curled in natural waves.

"I really enjoyed the service, Rev. Sloan."

"Thank you. Please, call me Peggy. I hope we will see more of you."

"I'm interested in attending your silent retreat next weekend. Are there still openings for it?"

"Yes, there are a few. The best thing would be to sign up today. Georgia, would you take Casey to the bookstore where they are doing the signups?" Georgia nodded. "I will look forward to seeing you next weekend then, Casey."

After signing up for the retreat and paying for it, Peggy and I went to the fellowship hall, where there was a buffet of food arranged. People gathered at tables after serving themselves, and there were all kinds of conversations, hugging, and laughter going on. Georgia and I joined a table with four other women, and all of them introduced themselves and welcomed me to the church.

When the other women returned to their conversation, Georgia said, "I'm glad you signed up for the retreat. I think you will really enjoy it. Peggy has been putting it together for a couple of months." I asked her if she would be going to the silent retreat. She shook her head. "No, I'm actually going to be speaking here that Sunday."

"Darn! Too bad I can't be in two places at once. I would enjoy being here to support you."

"You can go online at the church website, and they will have it there. I appreciate the thought, and I always feel your support."

***

In the middle of the week, I went to visit my hospice family, the Fitzgeralds. Morgan had been able to convince her mother to go out and have her hair done and for them to go to lunch. It was a big step of trust for Mabel to leave her husband and showed her confidence in having me there to stay with him. I made sure they had my phone number before they left.

Henry hadn't been eating for a couple of days. I moistened his mouth with a washcloth and put some lavender-scented lotion on his feet and hands. There were some old songs I sang to him, and his mouth moved along with the words a few times. His eyes followed me. He seemed to be relaxed. I didn't see any signs of him being restless or agitated.

When Henry closed his eyes, I made myself a cup of coffee, and then I retrieved a book from the bag I carried with me. It felt so peaceful sitting in a chair close to his bed. I was grateful to be able to spend this time with him and grateful Mabel had decided she could leave for a couple of hours with Morgan.

My thoughts gravitated toward Simon and our conversation about my volunteer work. I knew it was hard for him to understand how much giving a couple of hours of my time here and there meant to me. I knew this was something not everyone could do, and I was grateful to be someone who could. I felt like it was a privilege to serve these families as they encountered the challenges of watching someone they loved prepare for a different kind of journey.

I still hadn't heard or seen anything of Simon for almost a week. I didn't expect everything to come to a complete halt, but I knew that if the relationship was ended, it was best for both of us.

When Mabel and Morgan returned, Mabel looked pretty with her gray hair curled, and she had some color in her cheeks.

"Is everything all right with Henry?" Mabel asked as she went toward the bed. She put her hand on his cheek and then touched his hand.

"He was awake for a little while, and then he went to sleep. He is fine."

"I'm grateful you were here with him, Casey." Her blue eyes filled with tears. "I felt guilty for not staying home, but I have to admit, I did enjoy myself. Morgan and I haven't been out to lunch in a very long time. We used to enjoy doing that."

I gave her a gentle hug. "Henry would probably be glad you took some time for yourself, Mabel."

Mabel took some money out of her purse and offered it to me. "I want you to have this."

"Thank you for offering, Mabel, I appreciate it. I'm grateful to be able to do this for you and Henry, and I would rather you give the money to hospice as a thank you, at some time, if you want to. I love giving of my time as a gift to you. It means a lot to me."

***

On Friday morning, I looked again at the list of suggested things to bring for the retreat that had been emailed to me. They had also sent a map of how to find the retreat center where the silent retreat was going to be held. It suggested layers of clothes, because of the cooler weather outside, and comfortable walking shoes. I laid out the clothes on the bed, a flashlight, toiletries, and a journal. I had made some trail mix of things I liked to munch on and added that to the items I had gathered.

I felt nervous about going with a bunch of people I didn't know, and yet, inside of me, I knew this was something I wanted to do. I had no idea why I felt called to go, but I was willing to do it. If nothing else, I would be experiencing the energy of others as we were in silence together.

PART 4

Chapter 17

I arrived at the retreat center at four thirty and left my things in the car until I found out where my room would be. There had been a choice of sharing a room with someone else or to have my own room. I had elected not to share. I realized it was important for me to be alone for this time, when we weren't gathered as a group.

There was a lot of laughter and hugs being shared. I recognized a couple of people I had met at church the previous Sunday, but I couldn't remember their names. I was grateful to have them share their names again with me.

Rev. Peggy came up to me and greeted me with a warm hug. "I'm so glad you came, Casey. We are going to have some wonderful experiences together. Have you ever been to a silent retreat before? Although I have to admit, it isn't very silent right now," she added with a laugh as her eyes traveled a little around the room and then back to mine.

"No, I haven't. It will be a new experience for me, but I'm looking forward to it."

"After everyone has arrived, registered, and found their rooms, we will gather for our evening meal together. Afterward, we will go into the chapel for a service, and then we will officially be starting the silence."

I picked up the directions to my room and a key after signing in. The woman in the room adjacent to mine was coming out of hers, and she introduced herself to me. "Hi, I'm Cindy. I don't remember seeing you before. Are you new?" Cindy was about my own height, with short, curly red hair and shining hazel eyes. Her smile was wide and welcoming.

"Sunday was my first time coming to the church. When I heard about the retreat, I decided to come. My name is Casey."

"It's nice to meet you. Would you like to walk together to the dining hall after you get settled?"

"Thanks, I would enjoy it."

When Cindy left, I unlocked the door to my room and went in. The room was cozy, without frills with a double bed, a wooden dresser, and a small desk. Sliding glass doors led out to a small patio. Towels were on the foot of the bed, along with a stack with sheets and a warm blanket. I took the towels into the bathroom and made up the bed before going to the car for my belongings.

I stepped out on the patio when I was finished and breathed in the cool, fresh air. Pine trees were close by, and I could smell their familiar fragrance. I didn't know exactly why I was here, but I was willing to allow myself to be with it. I felt peaceful, knowing instinctively this was where I was supposed to be right now.

Cindy tapped on my door, and I went to open it. "Are you ready?"

"All I have to do is put on my coat," I answered as I snuggled into my warm coat, scarf, hat, and gloves.

"I forget that it can be cold here too," commented Cindy, "even though they are at a lower elevation than we are. I wonder if we will get some snow. Sometimes that happens during the retreat. I've been coming to the retreats since Rev. Peggy started having them a few years ago, and I've never been disappointed."

"I haven't been to a silent retreat before and don't know exactly why I decided to come. When it was announced on Sunday, I knew it was calling me. I live alone, so I'm used to having the quiet."

"I hear you. This is something I crave because of the constant noise in our household. My husband and I have three children, and quiet is challenging to find. And," she added with some emphasis, "quiet isn't really the same as silence, and you probably already know that. Being in the silence with a group of people is profound. It raises the energy vibration, and the love is palpable."

We arrived at the dining hall. It was filled with the buzz of friendly chatter, hugs, and greetings. I saw some of the women I had met at church. Cindy knew them, and we made our way to the big, round table they were standing near. A couple of chairs had not been claimed, so we took off our coats, hung them on the back of the chairs, and started returning hugs and joining in on the chatter.

Before the end of the meal, I was beginning to feel at home being with these women. We walked to the chapel and found seats together.

As Rev. Peggy took her place on the platform, the chatter stilled. She stood quietly, a smile on her face, with a loving gaze traveling to each one of the participants. When Rev. Peggy started to speak, she invited us into prayer and afterward presented the guidelines for the retreat. There were six people who had volunteered to be chaplains at the retreat if something came up for us where we wanted extra support, and she introduced these people to us. One of them was Cindy.

Rev. Peggy encouraged us to journal at times, to allow the thoughts and words to flow, and then to put it away without reading back what we had written in the journal. She also recommended we not read anything while we were here—no texting or emails—and to respect the silence by turning off all our electronic devices. Yoga and Tai Chi would be available both mornings. We would break the silence at ten o'clock on

Sunday morning with a special service and then share a meal together before returning home.

A few people had questions, and Rev. Peggy answered those before giving a brief message about the silence. She ended with a poem I had heard before called "I Am There," by James Dillet Freeman.

I Am There

Do you need Me?
I am there.
You cannot see Me, yet I am the light you see by.
You cannot feel Me, yet I am the
power at work in your hands.
I am at work, though you do not understand My ways.
I am at work, though you do not recognize My works..."

Peggy completed the poem, and she let us know copies of the poem would be handed out at the end of the retreat. I was grateful to hear that, because I was sure I no longer had a copy of it.

I would like to say being in the silence was a piece of cake for me, but it wasn't. Until I chose being in the silence, I didn't realize how much I talked to myself out loud or would fill the quiet with the television or radio. Once I became aware of it, it helped me to think to myself, *Peace* or *Thinking*. Eventually, as I would sit or walk or spend time in my room, I was able to just smile and think, *Isn't that interesting.*

It became apparent to me Friday evening as I sat journaling that I was carrying some anxiety about my relationship with Simon. The anxiety had not been conscious with me until I was alone and spending time in meditation. When I was busy with my friends, volunteering with hospice, or doing things at home, I had been able to put thoughts of him aside.

The word *surrender* flowed from my pen, and I knew I needed to let go of my feelings and to allow whatever was going to happen to happen. I desired the best thing for both Simon and me, and if letting the relationship go was the best thing, then that is what I wanted. I did not want Simon to change or become something he was not. Him attempting to change for me would not be the basis for a loving, lasting relationship.

On Saturday morning, Cindy and I came out of our rooms at the same time. We hugged and then walked together to the dining hall. It seemed like a different room this morning. The same faces were there, but there was no chatter or laughter. We hugged and bowed to each other with our hands held prayerfully over our hearts. It is hard for me to describe the way the energy felt, and my heart felt lighter and free.

After breakfast we gathered to meditate for an hour in the chapel and then went outdoors to do a walking meditation that was slow and contemplative. As we walked, a light sprinkling of snow was falling.

I journaled for a while and then took a short nap before lunch.

By Sunday morning I was sorry the retreat was about ready to come to completion. We meditated together as a group for half an hour, and then soft music started to play. No one spoke as we listened. When Rev. Peggy stood behind the lectern, she didn't say anything at first but allowed her gaze to lovingly flow from one person to the other. Then she said very quietly, "And so it is."

And as a group, we answered quietly, "And so it is."

Chapter 18

Most of the snow had melted, except for in shady places, as I drove home. I had left the radio off in the car, and neither did I listen to CDs. I enjoyed the quiet and being able to look at the clouds and scenery around me. I felt peaceful and wasn't ready to allow the outside world to intrude.

When I drove into my driveway, I stopped for a moment to drink in the sight of my lovely home I had created with love and the support of good friends. It was good to be home.

After unpacking, and starting a load of clothes, I picked up my phone. I realized it was still turned off. I hadn't even checked for messages while I was gone because I knew Georgia, Peter, and Jacob all knew where I was, and none of them would be calling. Georgia knew how to leave a message at the retreat center if there was an emergency.

I turned on the phone and was alerted to a text message and voice mails. Rather than taking care of them at that moment, I made myself some coffee. I wanted to take a few moments before rejoining my life. I was grateful to be able to come back into the busyness of my life in my own way. I was grateful

I didn't have a husband and a bunch of kids fired up and ready for me to jump back into all of the family activities and responsibilities. I thought of Cindy and smiled. Her return to life after the retreat would be totally different than mine.

There was a phone message from Hospice of the Pines. Diana had called to ask me to call the Fitzgeralds about changing my visit date with them, if possible.

The other voice mail was from Simon. "Hi, Casey. I texted and didn't hear back from you, and I haven't seen you coming and going. I just want to make sure you are okay. I would like to talk with you. I apologize for not asking sooner. I hope to talk to you later. If I don't hear from you, then I will check with Georgia to make sure you are all right. It doesn't seem like you would just stop talking to me altogether. Bye."

Simon's text asking for us to get together to talk had come yesterday morning, and his call was last evening.

Before calling Simon, I called the Fitzgeralds and found out Mrs. Fitzgerald had a doctor's appointment on Tuesday, and they wondered if I could visit with Mr. Fitzgerald while they were gone. "I will be glad to come," I said. We set up the time, and I wrote it down on my calendar.

I poured myself a cup of coffee and called Simon. "Hi, Casey," Simon said, "Did you enjoy your retreat? I spoke to Georgia, and she told me where you were. I hope you don't mind."

"No, I don't mind. I have fresh coffee, if now is a convenient time for you to talk and you would like to come over."

Fifteen minutes later, I opened the door to Simon, and he greeted me with a hug. "It's good to see you." He took a step back and looked at me. "I don't know what it is, but there's something different about you.

"Thanks for having me over, Casey," he added seriously. "After spending some time thinking about my past behavior, I realized I was way out of place trying to tell you what you should be doing, and acting like I knew what was best for you. I was afraid I had really blown any chance of a friendship, much less a relationship with you.

"I talked to Dave about it, and he was able to help me look at what might be driving my thoughts. It helped me a lot. Then I went over to Georgia and Dave's and had dinner with them. Georgia listened when I told her what Dave and I had been talking about.

"Georgia told me you are not some damsel in distress who needs a white knight to come on his big white horse to save you. Nor, she told me, are you a fragile piece of china that needs to be handled with kid gloves. She said what you deserve is someone to celebrate you for being the strong, courageous, compassionate person you are.

"So," he continued as he lightly beat upon his own chest and grinned, "I guess my Mighty Mouse imitation of, 'Here I am to save the day,' isn't the right thing for you. I hope you will accept my apology."

"Absolutely, Simon." I put my arms around him, and we held each other for a few moments, and then we kissed. I chuckled. "I will be glad to let you know if Mighty Mouse needs to rescue me."

He followed me into the kitchen and took the cup from me after I had poured him some coffee. "Tell me about this retreat. Were you really silent for a whole weekend? I don't mean to doubt you, but it seems like that would be a really hard thing for anyone to do. I can't imagine being silent for that long."

I laughed. "I had the same problem after signing up for it because I had never done it before," I admitted, "but I knew it was something I wanted to do. And I did it." I went on to explain what the retreat had been like, how I had to work on quieting my busy mind, and how I came to realize how much I was used to talking to myself. "I can laugh about it now. I thought living by myself I was in the quiet all of the time, but it wasn't true.

"I know you said you spoke to Dave and Georgia. What else have you been up to?"

He smiled. "I had a kind of restless night thinking about my conversation with Georgia and almost decided to stay home this morning, but I didn't. Dave picked me up, and we went to church together. Dave usually goes when he isn't on call for work, and when I found out Georgia was speaking, I wanted to go. I met your friends Peter and Jacob. They were there too. We all went out for lunch after church when Georgia was finished with all she had to do."

"I'm so glad you finally met them."

Simon nodded. "Me too. You have some wonderful friends."

"They say it takes a village to raise a child, and I may not be a child, but it has taken a village of loving, caring people to bring me to the place where I am today. Little by little, I have added more to my village. It's amazing to me that I once felt so alone and hopeless."

"I hope you will come to consider me as a part of your village, Casey."

"I already do, Simon."

He took my hand and held it gently. His green eyes gazed at me as if I was a valued treasure. "I feel like, I too, have expanded my village since I came to know you. After speaking with Georgia last evening, I felt like I had screwed things up with you." I squeezed his hand, and he continued. "I was really afraid there wasn't going to be any kind of relationship."

I smiled at him. "Simon, I'm not asking you to change or to be something you aren't. You are special, and I'm grateful to have you in my life."

He shook his head. "I'm not hearing you say that I need to change. There is something within me that is calling out for a new perspective. I'm not sure exactly what it means, but I believe you have been a catalyst for me to see some things differently in my life."

***

On New Year's Eve day, two years after we met, Simon and I drove to the Grand Canyon together. Snow was gently falling, and it felt like a different world to me than the one I had been in the last time I was here. We didn't do a lot of talking along the way, and yet, the silence was filled with love, peace, and joy. Every so often, Simon would look over and smile at me and gently squeeze my thigh or arm.

We arrived at the big lodge, and soon after, two other vehicles joined us. Our village walked with us to one of the nearby overlooks to the canyon.

"Dearly beloved," Georgia began, "we are gathered together in this wonderous space of God's creation to join this man and this woman ..."

Printed in the United States
By Bookmasters